The Carriage Driver

by

Michael Friedman

Mockingbird Books and Publishing

ISBN-10: 0986011452
ISBN-13 978-0-9860114-5-0

Dedicated to

Katie C. Friedman

and

In Memory of

Albert and Anthony

Introduction

I was inconsolable when my first cat died. At the age of sixteen, I needed my mom to explain the process of death. I wanted answers - specific answers.

In her usual manner, Mom listened to my fears. She asked me to think of Peppi's happiest days. Then she told me that heaven is a recreation of our most joyful time in life.

I've never forgotten this wise life lesson in my career choice of nursing - over thirty years ago. Working with patients and loved ones at times of death and grief is an emotionally charged labor of love.

All involved are dealing with any number of issues and feelings including anger, fear, blame, guilt, insecurity ~ at times, even a spiritual distress.

As a holistic nurse, I encourage patients, family, and students to tell their story. As I listen to the stories of others, I am frequently awed by the universality of our experiences.

As a writer, I've seen positive benefits in the fictional genre. A well-crafted story has the power to change one's experience of reality. We have the ability to use the very images, colors, and sounds that are created with the writer's pen to become more peaceful and centered. A release of feelings, fears and tears can accompany acknowledgment of the simultaneous grief and happiness in our life cycle.

"The Carriage Driver" stories by Michael Friedman exemplifies the healing powers of a story.

The Carriage Driver and his regal horse companion, Nuelle, are a metaphor for our last earthly journey.

Adaptability and compassion are a constant throughout each chapter. Every passenger has their own life story and vision of what the next life means to them. The wounds of a lifetime disappear. Miracles happen as a new reality is custom made with Friedman's masterful pen.

I invite you to make a book about *death* part of your *life*. Explore your own self-meaning, purpose and thoughts on spirituality, as you reach for this classic volume time after time.

I invite you to share a copy of *"The Carriage Driver"* with someone in your life in need of faith, hope, and peace.

Maria Jordan, Author, Nurse, Teacher
Jeffersonville, PA

Foreword

A gifted author of short story fiction, *The Carriage Driver* is a genuine Mike Friedman masterpiece. His keen insights into human nature and the world in which we live resonate with a universal appeal that is remarkable. With boundless imagination, Mike kidnaps the reader, taking us to the streets of Boston and the lives of ordinary people as they embark upon diverse, extraordinary journeys to the "other side." More than a collection of stories, this anthology instills a profound sense of awareness and feeling -- from the external landscapes of life to the mystical, holistic paths of self-discovery. Each story is brilliantly crafted, with a memorable cast of characters and unique, "we-are-there" visceral imagery and magnetism that keeps us turning the pages, wanting more.

Excellent writing doesn't get any better than this. A timeless classic, *The Carriage Driver*, will inspire and entertain readers who love great stories, well told, for years to come.

Genna Eastman

Preface

We are all led to believe that there is life after death. Western religion in all of its forms advises us so. Eastern religions have their own versions, and many promises are made in these religions as well. No matter the religion or continent of the world, promises have been made.

The *hereafter* or *afterlife* holds many mysteries for all of us. There does not seem to be any clear measure of what lies ahead. This work presents the instances where a person's life has led to a promised land.

We are all familiar with images of the boatman in a dark pool with a shrouded body with its eyes covered with coins, carrying a soul to the land of the dead. The skiff glides into a murky gloom and drifts silently into the unknown that waits across the river Styx.

The Carriage Driver requires no money; he waits patiently for all those that have gained admittance to the next higher life. The concept is simplicity itself. The Carriage Driver with his beautiful and intuitive white mare Nuelle provides passage. If the passenger wishes to wait for a loved one, there is a castle in the sky whose spires puncture heaven to accommodate them.

Those that have avoided the gates of hell have obviously gained special privilege. These stories explore those privileges. The old man and the stillborn child decide to return as twin brothers. The homeless woman decides to wait at the castle for her son's turn before they continue on. When it is the turn of a husband and wife of half a century who were born the same day, hour, and minute to go, they choose to ride the back of a whale with Ursa Major as their guide to the heavens.

The setting is Boston, with all of its history. But there are Carriage Drivers in all cities, towns, boroughs and villages. These stories bring us hope; they inspire what is good in us, and they are meant to make you think about the setting of your hereafter. Take pause, Nuelle and The Carriage Driver are waiting for you and your loved ones.

Table of Contents

The Carriage Driver - The Eliots

The frosty Boston night air was filled with the tolling bells of Old North Church. The carriage driver saw the couple in the distance just dark specs heading in his direction. The white mare's ear twitched in the frigid air. He and the mare were patient; there was no hurry. The street lamp illuminated the carriage in a halo of light.

The couple lumbered forward, crunched tightly together wearing their thick coats and their knitted caps and mittens. They stopped a few paces from the white mare and seemed to whisper to each other. Then they stepped closer, "Hey Mister," the woman's breath filling the air in front of him with steam, "how much for a ride?"

"Climb on up folks. There is a thick blanket on the floor, feel free to use it." Nuelle's ears twitched as she waited for the couple to get settled. She waited for the light movement of the reins, and she would begin to press her weight against the harness. Her hooves clicked and clopped against the icy stone path.

Mary spoke in a low voice, "John you have to promise me," she began. She clutched her mittened hands around John's as they huddled together. "You promise me that no matter what you will take care of the children."

"The children?" She heard him say. "Mary, our baby, is now twenty-seven years old. They don't need taking care of."

"They are going to need you to be stronger than you have ever been." Mary insisted. "You promise?"

Nuelle pulled and was glad to be moving. The stars rained full against the snow drenched streets, and John focused on the whispering air. He reached over and wedged the blanket tightly between the seat and Mary's leg. He put his hand to her face.

She heard the words, "I promise."

Over the years, she had learned that John strived to keep his promises and she was reassured.

She thought she recognized the corner of Battery Street as they made their way further along the path.

"This town is so rich in history. John, Michael is going to need you the most. He is grown but is still such a child at heart. You are going to need to speak to him differently from now on. I know he doesn't come around much. Not for a long time now. But he will. You'll see." Mary thought about tomorrows. When the golden moon appeared, she blinked hard. "John?"

John stared out across an untamed vista rugged yet beautiful. Nuelle whisked her long white tail which was the envy of the last wigmaker in Boston. The wheels clattered on the cobblestones of the long curving entrance to a castle whose spires punctured heaven.

"Where are we?" Mary asked the driver.

"We have arrived, and Nuelle needs to be fed and rested. Step down, please."

"It will just be a moment, or two and I will get us on our way."

Both John and Mary climbed down. The wide double doors of the castle entrance opened outward towards John and

Mary, and a tall, slender man walked through. "This way, please. You will be able to warm yourselves by the fire."

Mary clutched at John's arm walking wide-eyed and fascinated by her surroundings. The tall man walked through a stone archway and led them to a table near the hearth. He paused, "May I have your coats. I'll hang them right near the fire, and they will be dried and warmed when you are ready for them again."

Mary and John scooted their arms from their bulky coats and the coats where hung in sight of the fire.

"Please have a seat." He pulled the chair closest to Mary, and she took her place. John seated himself, his curiosity and his nervousness tugging at the forefront of his mind.

A slender man dressed in a tuxedo came through a side entrance and set a plate of brisket stuffed with oysters and bacon, and sprinkled with ground clove and nutmeg in front of John. Mary was served white lake perch with lemon and Worchester sauce covered with lemon slices resting on a slice of deep fried crouton. Fluted glasses were filled with ambrosia.

Mary watched John's face as he looked around. But the decision was made. He picked up his fork and began eating. Mary followed suit but with less gusto. She sipped her wine and inwardly smiled. Mary did not know if the music in her heart came from her heart or a room off to the entrance the server had used.

They ate in peace. John watched the steam lifting from their damp coats and wondered about the carriage driver. They finished their meal, and the server whisked away the plates. A woman in white carried two small plates and set them in front of her guests.

The aroma of Campari meringue and baked peaches with a raspberry sauce filled the air and delighted their senses. Mary watched John lift his glass; she did likewise, and the tapping of crystal echoed. John's smile always had an uplifting effect on Mary.

Through the same door, the servers had used, came three musicians with their instruments. They began to play. Both guests turned towards them while holding their Jacobean patterned china plates and their Tiffany sterling. Mary wondered if John saw the sparkling lights that lifted from the instruments and graced the air around her.

When Mary set down her plate, the musicians stood and walked back through the side entrance. The carriage driver walked through the front entryway. "Folks it is time to go. Nuelle is ready. She thanks you for your patience."

The tall, slender man entered through the side door and helped both his guests on with their toasty feeling coats.

At the entrance, Nuelle stood at her post in front of the carriage. "Climb in folks," the carriage driver offered. Once John and Mary were settled the carriage driver climbed into his seat and took hold of the reins and gave Nuelle a nudge.

Nuelle looked back over her shoulder. She began to pull; she pulled the carriage close to the stones of the castle and made a slow arching turn back the way she had come. The carriage driver sat up straight and gave her plenty of rein.

John and Mary craned their necks watching the castle recede into the wintry mist as the cobblestones made themselves heard under the hooves of the white mare.

The drifting snow seemed to dance as it swirled around the gas street lanterns and seemed to beam from its resting place on spruce and pine. Mary leaned her head on John's shoulder. His coat released some of its warmth into her. Nuelle now fed, and warm had a new bounce in her step, and she was anxious to get out of her harness and into her straw lined stall to sleep.

The carriage driver brought them to a stop and climbed down. He went to the side and held his hand out to Mary to help her out. Though her mittened hand, she felt a burst of warmth. John climbed down and reached for his wallet.

The carriage driver turned and climbed in, "Take me home Nuelle." Nuelle knew her way home; she liked this part of her journey the best.

It was the thirteenth hour of the nurse's twelve-hour shift. She walked into the waiting room. "Mr. Eliot." He was in deep prayer. "John, she is awake. She is asking for you."

The Carriage Driver – Mrs. Parker

It was a quiet day nearing evening. The carriage driver sat motionless and his white mare Nuelle was enjoying the last of the sun's rays. It was a slow day, but the carriage driver never worried. There were always customers.

The old man walked in silence thinking of his time. He walked up to the carriage and thought it was time. He climbed aboard startling the driver who was dozing. "Hello," the man said.

The carriage driver sat up straight and adjusted his eyes to the evening light. Nuelle stirred but did not take a step, waiting for her command.

"Hold on," the old man said. He looked across the grass of the park as a woman hurried towards them. She was carrying something, but at a distance, he could not make it out. When she arrived next to the carriage, the old man could see she was wearing scrubs and carrying a baby.

"Can he go with you?" She asked. "He should not go on his own." She paused, "Sir, please." She held the little bundle up, and the old man took it.

The old man put his finger on the edge of the blanket and peeked at the boy's face. "Well, boy it looks like it is you and me." His lips twitched at the thought.

Nuelle looked over her shoulder. This was most peculiar.

The carriage driver watched as the nurse walked off. "You settled back there?"

The old man looked up from his gaze into the bluest eyes he had ever seen. "Yes."

Nuelle felt the slightest movement of the reins along her side, and she stepped into the cobblestoned lane.

The old man adjusted the baby into the crook of his elbow and smiled at him. "I was so naïve when I was young. Believe me; there was no clue as to how things worked. Then a girl came along. I was infatuated with her. But if you were to ask me I would not admit it. Then I was rushed off to the service. Let me tell you that was an experience. The girl wrote, and I wrote, and before you know it, we were married. Yes, those were the times."

The baby's eyes went from the face of the old man to the blue of the sky. Peace filled his ears as the music of hooves clicked against the ancient stone of Beacon Hill along the Charles River. He could see the back of the carriage driver's head, and the aging silver studded leather upholstery.

"You didn't have time to know girls, did you? I can't tell you how much time is spent trying to figure out girls. Anyway, where was I? Oh, once my first child came along the perspective changed. The demands increased beyond belief. There was rent to be made and food to be bought and lawns to be mowed and bandages on knees and running alongside a bicycle." The old man smiled and adjusted the blanket. "You warm enough?"

To the musical score, came the sound of a train running along an old Boston and Albany line. Nuelle held her head high, the crisp air tousling her mane.

"There was never enough time. Sorry, I guess I cannot complain to you about enough time." He went on, "By the time my second daughter arrived the infatuation with the girl, well, it changed. It all changed. It was the darndest thing; there was a shift from need to want and it was all over for me." His head shook as he smiled. Well, I aged pretty fast after that. Then they were gone." The old man stared out at the river. He leaned forward being careful with the boy. "Where are we?" He called to the driver, but he didn't seem to hear.

The old man rocked the baby cradled in his arm, "Why you never even had a dog. Let me tell you about a dog I had. I retired and once I was home on a daily basis the dog never left my side. If I gardened, he would lay nearby. I began to talk to her, to even confide in her. That was a beautiful dog and, believe me, there was plenty of grief when she had to go. It's a crying shame you never even had a puppy kiss your face."

The carriage driver turned into the public gardens. Nuelle enjoyed the flowers and trees; the driver was aware of this, and he enjoyed the people walking through the park. At this hour, there were few people about.

The old man sat up straight seeing two young men throw a baseball in a game of catch. "Let me tell you a little about baseball. See those boys? Well, they are enjoying a catch. But the game, well, the game is where one man faces down eight men that are hell-bent on making sure he fails. It is an epic challenge where a man with a wooden bat tries to knock the ball past a gang of men practiced and trained to do everything they can to stop him. Many think it is a team sport, but the batter is alone in the batter's box. His teammates sit in the dugout in the shade waiting their turn to face the men on the field. Our town built a cathedral called Fenway Park to these men. Sure we have our churches, but nothing like this shrine. Thousands of people attend." He adjusts the baby's blanket. "Lots of young boys learn the rule of life while out on that field." A little tear came to the man's face. "Baseball teaches an abundance about failure and a little about success. Just like life. Ya know kid; you are an excellent listener."

Nuelle twitched her ear. The public gardens were the best part of this particular route. The carriage driver let the reins go slack giving Nuelle complete choice of the route and pace. He noted her pace had slowed. Partially because she was in the park and partially because the old man's voice was soothing to her ears. The branches of American elm formed a citadel of calm.

The face of the old man relaxed. He thought about his years. He thought about the baby in his arms. "You and I are going to be best friends, or better yet brothers. You are with me now." Leaning forward in his seat making sure not to squeeze the baby too tightly he said to the carriage driver, "Take us back."

Nuelle's ears twitched. She looked up ahead and saw a turn-about by the gazebo and made her way towards it. The twilight glittered her path. Her pace remained slow and steady; she loved the gardens. *Some things just seem to work out for a reason* she thought as her hooves clopped along the cobblestone passage.

The carriage driver lifted the reins. His smile displayed joy and good tidings.

~~~

Two nurses walked into her room. Each carrying a newborn boy in her arms.

"Here is Logan," said the first.

"And here is Ethan," chimed in the second. "It's feeding time, Mrs. Parker."
~~~

She often wondered where her publisher found the worn leather journals he kept supplying her with. He would arrive, give her a new journal as a gift and scurry around looking for a diary that was filled and rush off and set in motion another book. He would have a copy made and rush it to her illustrator who had done every title from the very first.

In the early days, the publisher sat and drank tea. He went through the proprieties of polite society and then scurried off with her latest journal. These days she hardly knew that he had arrived or taken a journal and left a blank journal. She sat and wrote. She made her tea and listened to music that made her soul tremble, and she scribbled her adventurous thoughts - rich and dark, creating tapestries of sanctuaries, and flowered pathways and lush valleys. Her bees would buzz, and her birds would sing as they flowed from her pen. She was both singular and universal.

Her writing room was simple. With the success of her second work of poetry, she took the funds and bought a hundred-year-old fold down desk and placed a modest lamp on it. Now fourteen books later the desk feels like hers and her hands are fragile.

Her illustrator took her words and garnished her pages with pastels of glimmering water, birds-on-the-wing, and youthful bodies casually draped. He drew vines climbing along trellises, peaches with a morning blush, anything as soft as her words as sweet as her thoughts. He rejected most of his work himself. He just kept tacking them all along the walls of his small studio. There were drawings of eyes so deep that you could walk right into them, there was sketch after sketch of the most delicate female forms. There were kittens and dancing muses, none ever good enough to make the pages of her books.

His hands had become gnarled and caused him pain. There were pastel crayons in cans. There were watercolor paint brushes lying in every nook and cranny and charcoals of every description. His publisher would arrive carrying a bag of groceries, which included coffee. He would set down a fresh supply of pens and Indian ink, crayons and he made sure each new color found its way into his toolbox. He would take what he needed from the walls and go join them with the words of his diarist.

The publisher gave himself credit - set in motion the outpouring of love flowing from his gifted flowers.

Her poetry titled, "The Inner Light of Her Eyes' was still selling copies after all these years.

Mission walls can be seen in the distance
and garden paths lead to emerald pools
resting after a morning swim
you ask yourself the meaning of happiness
and you rise and raise your face to the sun
noon turns to dusk as you walk through the meadows
night brings you dreams that see you safely to dawn

It was a warm Spring evening; she found herself outside walking along the commons. She wore a long flowing dress which was so common among the young girls with stars in their eyes. Her auburn hair caught the breeze as she skipped through the grass.

A young man walked along the commons; his dungarees bunched at the ankles were paint stained, as was his shirt and his fingers. His thick black hair was disheveled. His lean body moved with swagger. There was nothing rushed about him.

She watched him approaching with interest.

Nuelle's ears twitched as the Carriage Driver became aware of their approach. She was the first to arrive. Climbing aboard, she announced 'what a wonderful evening for a carriage ride,' loud enough for the young man to hear.

He stopped and looked up into her eyes. He wanted terribly to paint her from that very instant. "Can I share the ride with you?" He asked, climbing in before she had time to reply. "My name is Maxwell. I am usually very shy, but there is something about you…"

He did not finish his sentence.

"I'm Gene. I am a writer. I see so much in everything; I can hardly put my pen down. I hope to make my living writing."

"I hope to find a job where I can illustrate books." He made a face, "But no one will hire me without the proper experience."

At the Carriage Driver's light touch of the reigns, Nuelle pulled onto the cobblestoned street. The air was scented, and she thought to take the long way towards Wordsworth, then Byron Street, down Milton heading back up to Hogarth and Trumball near Breed's Island. The sea air drew her as strongly as fresh cut hay.

The couple sat chatting, and it was not but a moment before she took his hands in hers as they talked.

Nuelle whisked her long white tail as the wheels clattered on the cobblestones. She turned into the long curving entrance to a castle whose spires touched the sky. The wheels played a symphony as they moved along their path at a slow gate.

Maxwell scooted closer to Gene. Their legs touched. "Would you look at that castle? I never knew there was a Trumball Castle."

Nuelle did not stop, the couple watched as they passed the castle with sparks of lights dancing in the windows, and big inviting doors they felt sure hid mysteries.

"Wish I brought a pen and a journal, I could write all day just about such a beautiful entrance." She squeezed Maxwell's hand.

"I feel the same way. If I had a jar of Indian ink and a sketch pad, I could create a fairytale lane leading us to the safety of that castle. Surely there is music there."

Their heads turned as Nuelle continued on and the castle receded into the distance and the cobblestone orchestra laid down their instruments.

Both Gene and Maxwell turned and climbed to their knees on the seat and watched the sky and sea from above. Their senses were spinning magnets trying to absorb the energy and sights as they continued on.

The Carriage driver was an old hand at this trip. He often wished he could make the trip more often. The carriage and Nuelle leveled out as they reached the destination. She pulled to a gate that had swung open to reveal a beautiful garden. The birds and flowers and bees and trees that flowed through her poetry greeted her. The carriage driver climbed down and extended his hand to help first Maxwell then Gene climbed down.

Maxwell stared, he turned in a circle; he was sure that he had drawn everything before him. The garlands and vine-covered trellis, the singing bird-on-the-wing, and the happy bees. He had drawn the winking flowers and the colorful dragonflies and delicate female forms.

Maxwell and Gene turned and looked at the carriage drive. Gene took the two steps that separated them and embraced him. Maxwell seeing this also gave the carriage driver a hug who then climbed back onto the carriage and gave Nuelle the touch of the reigns as she began the journey home.

Maxwell and Gene watched a tall, lean man wearing a tuxedo approach the open gate. When he arrived, he said, "Follow me, please."

The two did just that. The man walked slowly allowing Maxwell to take in all the beauty of the garden and allowing Gene to compose in her mind. She said, "Max, I think we are on the other side of sunset."

The person leading them reached the door. He swung it open and waved the couple inside. The swinging of the door caused the members to put down their pens, or their books or papers or to stop typing and turn towards the door.

Upon seeing Maxwell and Gene in the doorway, every member in the room stood and began their applause.

The Carriage Driver - Engine 610

Nuelle, the white mare had not made a trip all day. Darkness swept across the Atlantic spreading gray in its path as the Carriage Driver dozed in his seat. Nuelle's ears twitched. She did not see anyone heading towards her. Nuelle, who was usually docile, anxiously stirred as she waited for a command. With the first whiff of smoke, Nuelle pulled from the curb without further waiting.

The crew of Engine 610 sat braced as they responded to a call of a three-alarm fire as the truck pulled out of the station and began their journey accompanied by a blaring siren. Each of the crew looked out into the darkness not knowing what the night would bring.

Nuelle pulled the carriage first at a trot as she picked up speed. She rushed along Chelsea Street past Winthrop Square toward the old Nashua & Lowell Railroad quays. Her hooves clicking along pulling the steel rimmed wheels as the driver was torn from his sleep wondering what events were unfolding. An orange glow rippled the skyline ahead. The driver sat up straight and took the reins in his hands as the smoke penetrated his conscience. He braced his legs to secure himself in his seat.

Young Jim Bailey was still considered a rookie by the rest of the crew. He was new to civilian life and this new station. He had things to prove to these men, and he meant to prove it. He was always first to be ready and onto the truck and always first to go through the door into the fire. The chief remained unimpressed and cautioned him about recklessness.

Nuelle reached a gallop towing the carriage. Her black rimmed nostrils flaring as she strained against the harness. She felt the weight of the carriage fighting her and she dug-in straining the breechings. A wheel popped onto a curb as she searched for running space jarring the driver who held tight to the reins, but not interfering in any way. People on the street turned and watched not knowing what to make of this runaway carriage.

Bailey had been jeered by his peers when he had his air-bourne wings engraved on the eye of his Seagrave axe; he just took it as good-naturedly as he could. Now he held that axe in his hand as he stepped from the rail of the truck at the scene of the fire. He and his partner were the first ones through the door of the flaming old three story building. The rest of the crew pulled the hoses from their coils and began spraying water and looked around for other trucks to arrive.

The crowd that always appears at fires began to gather across the street from the three-story building. Most just stared and shook their head. Police arrived to keep the crowds out of the way.

Inside on the top floor little Elizabeth Collins sat petrified clutching her doll. On the ground floor, Jim's partner saw an old man lying on the floor and rushed to him. "Anybody else in the house?" He screamed through his oxygen mask.

He helped the man up. At the same time, he heard his Captain through his headpiece say to evacuate the fire was too hot. Jim Bailey received the same message but seeing a picture of a young child in a frame on a table he rushed upstairs. He pushed open one door and did a quick search.

His partner made his way down the front steps dragging the old man along with him. Two police officers rushed to his side and led the man to safety. The partner turned to go back inside but was caught by the arm by his Captain.

"Where is Bailey?" He called out. "Damn that guy." Another truck arrived, and a flurry of men in full uniform descended and unfurled more hose and began to deliver rain. The Captain released the arm of the partner. "Bailey, do you hear me?" He screamed into the microphone. "The place is going to go, get out of there. Do you hear me, Bailey! Get out now. Number four, get a hose on the doorway and keep it there."

At the top of the stairs, Jim Bailey used his Seagrave axe and went through the last door with no trouble at all. He was muscular and young and to his mind unstoppable. He saw a little girl and rushed to her; stepping over flames; he scooped her up in his arms. He took one step then the floor gave. His grasp tightened around her as they tumbled. He felt a shadows embrace.

Nuelle reached the street of the three-story building at full gallop. She took the carriage up a curb to get around two police vehicles blocking the entrance to the street and in doing so ran over two fire hoses as she raced for the house. The carriage drive was jarred unmercifully as he took in the scene. A burning house, two full fire brigades, police and a crowd of onlookers surrounded him as he was being pulled towards the front of the house.

Every head turned towards the house as the sound of the collapsing roof clutched their attention. Nuelle was just a few turns of the wheel from the porch at street level when Jim Bailey with one boot on fire came through the front door at full throttle. In one arm was Elizabeth Collins; the flaming handle of the Seagrave axe was in his other hand. He bounded down the stairs, took three steps to the street, with a shadowy wake of fiery ash swirling after him like a serpent's tongue as he leaped, barely touching the carriage step, onto the back seat as it passed.

Fire laden ash, with no soul in hand, drifted to rest on the street as the crowd gasped at the sight and a volcanic plume spewed from the house towards the heavens as the roof fell through to the ground floor.

Nuelle's speed did not slow until she turned a corner and was out of sight of the crowd. She slowed; her breathing was heavy, and her coat glistened from the run. The carriage driver barely knew what to think. Nuelle's heart beat and the carriage driver's heartbeat began to slow.

Jim Bailey brushed the fire out on his burning boot, and Elizabeth's hair stopped smoldering. He took off his hat and oxygen mask and tossed them over the side. He looked at the carriage driver and Nuelle and the cobblestoned street and threw the now ember glowing hickory handled axe over the side as well as he sat back.

The Boston Globe spoke of their passing. It spoke of the fire. It spoke of those they left behind. It spoke of the proud history of Engine Company 610. It spoke of Jim Bailey's heroic but failed attempt to save Elizabeth Collins. There was no mention of Nuelle.

Nuelle watched with curiosity as the man wearing western garb limped straight towards her. He reached her and went into his vest pocket and produced an apple. He went to his other vest pocket and out came a folding knife that he used to cut the apple in half. He fed half to Nuelle and patted her cheek, just as The Carriage Driver was prone to do while he groomed her.

The man with the cowboy hat with the front brim pinned back took a bite of the other half of the apple and he and Nuelle shared a bond. He gave Nuelle the rest to finish and limped along the side of her and slapped her side.

The Carriage Driver watched with interest. His riders were generally anxious to climb aboard and see what was next on the journey. They arrived slowly and casually and generally boarded. They had achieved a level of peace within them that was predictable.

"Afternoon," said the man with the limp.

"Good afternoon, sir. Are you here for a ride?"

"My ride? I usually just throw a saddle on my horse and ride up high on his back, not sitt'n in back." He leaned against the front wheel. He was fix'n to chat awhile.

"Oh, said The Carriage Driver. "You walked up to the carriage – that usually means I have been sent a customer."

"I see," the man said shifting his weight. He reached into his pocket and pulled out a packet of tobacco. Then he rolled himself a cigarette and began smoking. "Want a smoke?" He asked looking keenly at the man in the driver's seat.

"No –No thank you." The afternoon sun and the salt filled air from the sea made the afternoon pleasant. "Not many people show up along this path. Nuelle sets a nice pace that many find very memorable. Are you sure you don't want to hop aboard?"

"I'm thinking about it. Where did you say you took your passengers? If ya mentioned it I, missed it." The long beard did not disguise his wise eyes. "You had this job long? You looked like you were sleeping as I came up to you."

"I had other jobs. But I am particularly well suited for this one. You can say I was hand-picked. Nuelle and I have worked together for many years. She could make the journey without me holding the reins. You say you have done some riding?"

"Me, yeah plenty. Last horse I had stood fifteen hands – I called him Big John. Ya know – Big John, like the old song – You must have heard it. *Big Bad John,* Maybe it was not so popular here in the city."

Nuelle waved her tail as she listened to the two men talk. She wished she was back at the stables, and they were giving her a proper brushing.

The man, getting into his stride said, "My granddaddy use to drive for Wells Fargo lines, the old Butterfield route. So, he was in a similar profession as you. He drove a carriage and carried a scattergun across his lap. I'm guessing you don't get much call for use of a scattergun. You ain't likely even packing a Colt .44 Magnum on your hip. Times have changed I'll tell you that for certain. Yes, sir. Oh, what was I talk'n about? I remember my last horse, half quarter horse, and half Percheron. She was a beauty. In our day, we explored the Sonora Desert together. Yes, sir."

"Sounds like a wonderful experience. I have read that the desert southwest is quite beautiful. But cities have their charm also."

"Charm, let me tell you about charm. Me and John on special occasions would ride into town to eat a big breakfast at a local Café. Half a dozen eggs, a half pound of bacon, a separate plate to hold French fries, a cream cheese Danish with lemon jelly topping and they made coffee that would hold a spoon stiffer than…Oh never mind that. Once breakfast was done, we could ride until sundown before making our way home."

"That's a lot of food. I am surprised I have not seen you earlier," the Carriage driver interjected.

"Where is everybody? This time of day, you would think there would be folks about. I ain't seen a soul since I came up on you. Reminds me of a time, when I was living in the desert. It was a completely quiet night when all of a sudden my two Rottweiler dogs went to rattling like it was The Lord himself returning that very minute. Since I wasn't expecting no company, I grabbed, "Old Bess," my double barrel 12 gauge stagecoach guard shotgun that I kept handy, in one hand and a stick I carved for a quick crutch in the other hand and go have a look-see.

A hungry Bobcat snooping around got a big surprise as those two dogs bolted passed me protecting the area where the chickens were roosting. I did not see those dogs again for two days. They come home happy as if they been on vacation at some Texas steak house. Never did see that Bobcat again." He took a breath, not wanting to take up all the conversation.

The Carriage Driver was leaning forward. He did not say anything.

The Cowboy began again, "I happened upon this fellow one-day sitt'n in his car under an old Mesquite tree reading old Zane Gray paperbacks. Charlie was his name, told me he had come out to the desert to die; a cancer had grapt hold of him, and he couldn't shake it off. I offered him some food and lodging if'n he cared to. At first, he turned me down. But I visited him every day, try'n to see to his needs. And the needs of an old black Terrier stray that he had taken to traveling with. We took that dog to my place, and I gave him a bath, turns out that dog after a couple of good scrubbings was as white as snow, so we got to calling him Snowball. My female Rotty's had so much fun being teased and growled at by this twenty-pound male. It was not long after that the fellow died. I had to call reach the authorities, and they came and took him and made a report. Shortly after Snowball passed and I buried him under the old Mesquite where I first met him."

The Carriage Driver began to understand how this fellow here arrived at the foot of his carriage. "You sure you don't want to climb on board? I can climb down and help you into the carriage if needed."

"Last time I just climbed on board something without asking a lot of questions the government whisked me off to Southeast Asia. Yes, sir – let me tell you that is certainly a ride that I am not going to get out of my system anytime soon. I was a young man then. That was long ago. My left leg is still there. Was told they gave it a Christian burial, but over the years, I become to have my doubts. We all came home adrenalin junkies from that excursion." The cowboy scratched at his beard, thinking. "Just before I decided to take this here walk, I read a poem and old fellow wrote forty years later, about us that went something like this...."

A Grand Day To Die A plea

I hope the day does not arrive
Where old soldiers are forced to
fight young soldiers, while half cows
are barbecued, and the greasy-jowled,
lick their fingers, and smile on the TV,
and talk about the morals of the country,
while they plunder behind the scenes,
and flaunt that they can plunder in front of the
scene because the firepower reports to them and
are paid with pieces of paper and promises,

I hope the day does not arrive
where a store bought smile and three
changes of starched shirts paraded in front of
the cameras and "my friends" comes out of
the mouths of those that know nothing of making
the choice between 'Top Ramen" and
"cup of noodles," and a slice of bread with
a little mold is eaten rather than wasted

I hope the day does not arrive
where twenty men die in pursuit
of a stash of weapons in the hands
of an old warrior and a notion that
the word freedom has meaning
and independence is a fact of life,
versus a notion in a textbook.

I hope the day does arrive
where a man, who when called
fought and paid a high price for
those that said "this is our fight."
A man who earned the rights that

he now holds precious and whose remaining time should be enjoyed on the land that he loves and he carries with him the pride he has rightly earned and his days are lived out in peace.

The cowboy stood tall, pushing himself off the wheel he had been leaning on. "Well, I guess I can't just stand here jawing all day. On the way over I saw a whole trainload of people laughing and whooping it up. It looked like a party was about to start. I think I will just mosey on over there and see if I can join up with that party. Great talking to you."

Nuelle turned her head and watched him go.

In memory of 50 Caliber.

Peace

The Carriage Driver – David's Trumpet

The air was so cold that the notes coming from David's trumpet could not fall to earth; they hung gently drifting, suspended tumbling amongst the invading snow. The glow of the street lights cast a spell of serenity that belied the desperation. The open trumpet case at David's feet contained a few coins and a hand full of snow. That was not enough to purchase a meal for his mother who waited beneath the old Eastern railroad crossing at Summer Street near Maverick Park.

Debbi Sauro lay wrapped in a blanket. She found herself on hard times when her husband passed away. She hated that David had to go and stand in the cold to play his trumpet for coins to feed them, but her search for work had turned up nothing. Piece by piece she had sold off her belongings. Then still unable to pay the rent, clutching her old coat to her breast in one hand and her twelve-year-old son David with the other, she closed the door of her apartment for the last time.

They wandered the streets for hours in search of a place to sleep. She decided on the abutment of the railroad overpass because of the concrete footing and protection overhead and from the east wind. Now two days later her spirits were at their lowest, and they had nothing to eat.

Nuelle stood with a blanket over her back, pinned at her neck to help shield her from the snow. The Carriage Driver draped a blanket over his legs, and his thick coat and hat gave him some protection from the elements. Nuelle's ear twitched as the notes from David's trumpet swirled along in the drift. The man lifted the reins and directed Nuelle to follow the notes like bread crumbs along Webster Street.

David lowered his horn and looked in both directions. Seeing no one, he scooped up the change in the trumpet case and put the trumpet away. Seeing an open market he walked over and purchased a package of Hostess Chocolate Cupcakes. One cupcake was for him and one for his Mom.

When he reached Summer Street, David was surprised to see a carriage with a white mare parked under the railroad tracks. He picked up his pace and was soon running toward what had been where he slept for the last two evenings. When he arrived at the carriage, he was surprised again to see his Mother sitting in the back.

Without hesitation, David climbed into the carriage and sat next to his Mom. "Mom, what is going on Mom?"

Nuelle waited a moment and at the nudge of her reins pulled the carriage on its journey. She would just have to trust The Carriage Driver.

David's big eyes widened as Nuelle whisked her long white tail as the wheels clattered on the cobblestones of the long curving entrance to the fantasy castle of his imagination. Nuelle stopped at a walk paved with smooth stones that led to two wide double doors.

A tall, slender man opened the doors wide in greeting. The Carriage Driver got down to help Debbie out; David hopped out by himself star-struck at the sight before him. "This way, please," offered the man wearing a tuxedo.

"I am going to feed Nuelle and then I will come back for you," the carriage driver told David, who was standing there holding his trumpet case.

"You can hang your coats by the fire if you like," offered the man tending the door. "They will be dry and warm when you are ready for them again." Then with a wave of his hand, he said, "Please take a seat while you are waiting."

David held out a chair for his mother, and she sat down, her heart now free from worry. David took a seat and absorbed the heat from the fire.

A woman wearing a white outfit set a plate with two generous cuts of herb-rubbed sirloin tip roast with garlic mashed potatoes and gravy and a scoop of green peas in front of Debbie and a glass of hot apple pie cider. She could not contain the tears forming in her eyes.

David was served the same meal with smaller portions and only a tablespoon of green peas. The two had begun to eat when an older gentlemen came through a different stone entryway and began to play trumpet. He finished one song, set his trumpet down and took a seat at the table with Debbie and David.

The server brought him a plate, and he joined them. "Your name is David, right?" He said with a coy smile. Debbie peered closely at the face of this guest. The man looked down at the side of the table, "Is that a trumpet case?" His voice was warm, and his face marked with lines from a life of smiling and playing his trumpet.

"Yes, that is mine. Well, it is borrowed, but I use it." David said reaching down and taking his trumpet from the case and removing the package of Hostess Chocolate Cupcakes he placed in the bell for safe keeping.

"Will you play something for us?" The man asked.

David lifted the trumpet and began to play, after a minute the man stood and retrieved his trumpet and went and stood by David and began to play.

David watched him closely. He noticed the man held his trumpet differently in his hand, and he noticed that he took deeper breaths at the pauses. And he shifted his hands on his trumpet and took deeper breaths.

When they had finished, there were people standing in all of the doorways that entered the room; they had all stopped what they were doing to listen to the performance. They applauded and disappeared back to what they were doing.

"That was fun," David told the man. "Thank you."

Debbie took a sip of her apple cider. The man and David went back to eating, as you all know men love to eat.

When they were finished with their meal, the server came and cleared their plates and offered desserts.

"Just some plates and a knife please," David smiled. When the plates and knife arrived, he opened the package of cupcakes and cut one-third from two of them leaving three remarkably equal portions. The three enjoyed their dessert together smiling.

The Carriage Driver returned and said, "David it's time to go."

David looked at his mother and ran to her and gave her an enormous hug. She leaned down and received kisses on both cheeks. He put his trumpet back into its case and gripped it tightly.

The old man said, "We will be waiting right here for you before we continue our journey. No rush, we will see you in seventy years."

Debbie took the old man's hand, and they walked together into a large lounge, to sit and catch up. She thought she recognized him.

"We just have to wait," Dr. Hammond, at Tuft Medical Center informed Mrs. Clark. "He is young, and we have a very good chance."

"Thank you, Doctor."

"You can bless your lucky stars. There were two on the waiting list in front of you, but we were unable to reach them in time," the surgeon at Boston Children's Hospital explained to the anxious parents after surgery.

"Thank you, Doctor."

"We have performed over a hundred of these operations," the tired surgeon at John Hopkins Hospital told the tired family after surgery. "We will know in a couple of days. But everything looks promising."

"Thank you, Doctor."

Three emergency vehicles raced from the exit drives from Mass General Hospital in Boston each carrying precious cargo. One each bound for Tuft Medical, John Hopkins Hospital, and Boston Children's Hospital. Their sirens cut the silence of the black cold night. The organ transplant system was working full tilt.

Once the teams of collaborating surgeons were assembled by the staff coordinator, hasty calls went out to the surrounding hospitals for them to consult their waiting lists of patients.

In surgery, the young, healthy eyes, heart, and kidneys were removed and put into coolers and loaded into waiting emergency vehicles.

His parent was contacted.

Boston Police requested an ambulance from Mass General. Neither driver survived the accident. The Ford lay on its side in the middle of the road. The Mercedes' driver's side smashed from impact with the Ford and the front end smashed from the second impact with a tree.

The officers stood in the cold, their patrol car lights flashing, directing traffic to alternate routes while pointing emergency teams to the scene.

Two firefighters used the Jaws of Life to pry open the Ford driver's side door and then pull the broken body from its resting place.

An Officer checked for id. He held up the license to the EMT, "Look, he's a donor."

The EMT screamed, "Joe, let's get him into the ambulance." To the Officer, "Another ambulance will arrive for the other driver." The two EMT's rushed him into the ambulance and with no regard for their safety raced towards the hospital.

The last seconds of his earthly time were punctuated by loud screeching smoking brakes. The Mercedes hurtling toward him sideways sliding along the black ice mingled with his last thoughts. His very last image was of her green eyes rushing towards him.

The last words in his mind were those of his father, "You are a failure. You will never amount to anything!" After downing his drink, he'd said, "That is the third job you have lost since you graduated High School. What is wrong with you? You think you are going to sit around here and eat my food, well you are sadly mistaken. Get out of my sight." Joey's dad screamed slamming down his empty scotch and coke on the coffee table.

Joey stood behind the counter at Haas Liquor Store. Mr. Meyers told him, "You see my nephew is coming to stay with us. My sister is having trouble with him. Anyway, I cannot afford both of you, and he is going to take your job. I can give you a reference if that is of any help. He starts tomorrow, come back for your check on Friday. I'll have it ready."

The carriage driver holding the reins watched as the young man approached. The young man appeared lost as he walked looking here and there hands buried in his pockets, in the carriage driver's direction.

Nuelle's white tail waved, and her ear twitched. Nuelle was cold, as she stood in the halo of the street lamp on this dark evening. She was surprised to be awakened at this early hour. Her harness gently applied, and a warm blanket rested over her shoulders.

"I seem to be lost," the boy told the carriage driver. "And I see sights that are not my own. I thought I was driving…" his voice faded.

"You are not lost," the carriage driver assured him. "Are you cold? There is a blanket in the back."

"Cold, no, I am not cold," the boy looked around trying to get his bearings.

The carriage driver watched, with curiosity, as a tiny figure appeared in the distant and seemed to be walking towards him.

The small spec grew into the silhouette of a young woman, then into the dimensions of a young woman. When she was near enough to the light, Joey shivered as he made out the woman with green eyes. He knew her from somewhere.

"Thank you for waiting," she told him. "I was sent for you, but you arrived here first."

Joey smiled; he glanced up at the carriage driver then back at her. "Sent for me? What an odd thing to say."

"Why don't you climb on board?" The carriage driver said in a tone so welcoming that Joey put his foot on the step and pulled himself on board.

The green-eyed woman's head tilted back looking up at the young man, "I have come a long way for you."

At the slightest touch of the reins, Nuelle began to pull the carriage. The sound of her hooves was soothing to Joey. The woman stood at the curb watching the carriage pull away. "Grab the blanket and draped it over your legs. It will keep you warm," the carriage driver called over his shoulder.

Joey leaned forward, "Man, where are you taking me?" He looked around seeing images that were not there, and images there. He rubbed his eyes.

Nuelle pulled down a street filled with flashing blue and red lights. As they approached Joey could see a Ford lying on its side surrounded by broken glass. Four men were rocking the car, to push it back onto its wheels to be towed away. A Mercedes crumpled and battered was being hauled on a flatbed tow truck. Joey's jaw went slack; he thought he recognized his car.

Joey's old man sat in the dark. After receiving the call, he had refilled his Scotch and coke for the third time. There were tears in his eyes as he sat in the dark trying to remember the last words he spoke to his son. But he could not remember. He knew they were angry words; words said to hurt, and he wanted them back. But they were there echoing through the murky walls of his mind. He realized that now he was empty and alone - he and his words and his scotch.

The mother of the girl who received young, healthy kidneys was on her knees praying in thanks for the gift of life her daughter received. The recipient of the heart transplant lay in the cold, dim, hospital room talking to his new heart, welcoming his new heart and promising to give thanks every day for this chance for him and his family.

The mother sat at the side of her daughter with brand new eyes. They sat patiently waiting the removal of the bandages from her face. Once the bandages were removed, she blinked her eyelids then said, "Momma, I have seen heaven."

The Carriage Driver - The Pianist

Lisa Marie Young was by all measures a frail person. Yet seated in front of her piano on the top floor of the Boston Conservatory she was a giant. Her long pale, graceful fingers glided over the keys like a polished Newell Boathouse crew along the smooth Saint Charles. She would often practice in the dark on the top floor with the windows wide open. While she practiced her art, her music escaped into the night floating upon primordial airstreams penetrating souls of artists and lovers throughout the area.

She was told her upcoming concert at Jordan Hall was sold out. She had performed there years ago. The acoustics elevated the music into a transcendent realm filling the listeners with the sublime to the point they felt their hearts would burst.

She trained and practiced on her beloved and locally manufactured Mason & Hamlin. But for her next public performance she was offered and accepted to have the use of a Fazioli belonging to one of the Boston Brahmins. Fazioli's she was told, were sculpted, not manufactured and exuded majestic projection.

She sat and composed; she jotted notes on her Passantino Manuscript paper. She played the notes, erased, jotted and played them again. Then to relax she would play Billy Joel and often garnished the air with Dustin O'Halloran. In late spring and summer, the young would spread blankets on the grass off the Emerald Necklace and shared the music with the stars as they drifted off to sleep in each other's arms.

Nuelle stood in her stall. The Carriage Driver had finished up with the Currycomb and Dandy brush and now used body brushes in each hand as he continued grooming Nuelle in preparation. He was spending extra time today. He intended to stand on a wooden crate and comb every bit of her long white mane. Nuelle preened. Once he finished with Nuelle, he planned to spend his afternoon cleaning the carriage, polishing the leather seats and the tackle. He had extra time, but he wanted things to look their best.

There was an uncommon bustle in many of the homes in Beacon Hill, Back Bay and Fenway-Kenmore the evening of her performance. The Abbott's and the Amory's and the Webster's have all looked forward to this extraordinary evening out. The men donned their Brioni or Zegna suits while the women adorned themselves with Bergdorf Goodman or Monique Lhuillier gowns. This, after all, was the place to be seen. The jewelry came out of their safes and the Mercedes and Rolls-Royces, and minority Lincoln-Continentals were polished.

The night of the performance had arrived. For a quarter of a mile in both directions of Jordan Hall, Gainsborough Street was decorated with festive lighting. The red carpet had been rolled out by the city to honor Lisa Marie Young.

A procession of gleaming vehicles dropped off their passengers, and their chauffeurs or valets whisked them away. Boston's Sovereigns made their way to their seats as the hour neared. The 989 cushioned permanent seats were filling rapidly.

Nuelle pulled to the curb in front of Jordan Hall after the rush of cars had slowed to a trickle. Her five passengers climbed down; four women dressed in white with full white cloaks extending to their ankles the one male dressed in a crisp black suit. They entered and made their way to the first row, Section A Balcony seating.

A young valet offered the carriage driver valet parking. He smiled and declined, telling the boy he would get his chance to have a carriage ride in the distant future. Nuelle pulled away from the front of the theater and found a place to wait.

The house lights dimmed and went back on announcing that the performance was to begin. The curtain opened, and the house stood and applauded the entrance of Lisa Marie.

In the balcony, a young man dressed in a crisp black suit rose, the women in white sitting on each side of him reached over and took his arms and gently guided him back in his seat. His face had a quizzical look on it as he sat back down.

The Pianist took her seat and began to play. The already hushed crowd became silent as her music washed over them, rained down on them and cleansed their spirits. The audience became as rustling kelp in a sea with a light current. Many of the women gripped the arms of their seats for fear of floating into the air. Many others were bathed with exaltation as they felt their very essence exposed.

Notes danced along the backs of chairs, and across balcony rails. Notes danced over the tops of feet and down the aisles and along bare arms. They tiptoed up behind ears and across necks and down bare backs. They touched and caressed, and made mischief. The musical notes the Pianist let free into the hall formed columns as would an invading army marching across empty fields towards hungry hearts.

As the first piece finished, the audience was on its feet. Their applause shook the hall. Lisa Marie stood and took a quick bow. Her heart rate accelerated; as the conduit of the music she carried the most current, becoming General to the first wave of the army she just released.

As she continued her performance, she could see a woman wearing a long white cloak standing next to her piano. She diverted her attention from the audience and in a state of ecstasy, began releasing her army of notes towards her.

As the music continued, the remaining women draped in white billowing cloaks appeared with her on stage. They remained with her through the rest of the concert. The walls and roof of Jordan Hall were tested that evening – Lisa Marie raised the roof.

After the last bow, the curtains closed. The doors of the theater exhaled the satisfied women and their counterparts back into the city. The remaining musical notes drifted into the evening air. Busy valets and chauffeurs whisked away their charges.

In the new found, quiet Nuelle brought the carriage around to the front of the theater and waited.

Lisa Marie sat in a dressing room feeling frail. She was not the giant of a woman that appeared on stage fortified by her instrument. She heard the tap at the door and stood to open it.

The most handsome man she had ever seen stood there in a crisp black suit. He smiled a lighthouse-bright smile that made her glow. She reached out her arm, and he took it. He led her into the theater, down the red-carpeted aisle towards the front entrance.

There was elegance about the scene. The carriage was polished bright. Nuelle's coat glowed, and her ear twitched, and her white mane waved in a light breeze. Lisa Marie felt the magic of the evening.

She looked around wondering why the woman in white cloaks that she had seen on stage were not here to greet her.

The carriage driver climbed down and offered his hand to her as she and the man in the crisp black suit climbed aboard.

The carriage driver looked over his shoulder at the man in the crisp black suit; the look on his face asked the unspoken question, '*Where are they?*'

In a moment, a set of double doors opened, and the four women in white were there pushing the Fazioli piano.

"Ladies! Ladies, you cannot take the piano in the carriage. Can you put it back?"

In unison, the angels removed their cloaks and spread their wings. Each took a corner and lifted the piano flying towards the sky. "Meet you there," were the last words Lisa Marie heard on earth.

Patrolmen Joseph Warren Revere hated when he drew night shift. Still, after two years it never failed that someone at the station would wish him well on his midnight ride. He was often quoted and misquoted pieces of Henry Wadsworth Longfellow's poem. He felt it tiresome. His good-natured fellow officers had made being a descendant of a famous revolutionary like something to be lived down.

The thin, steady rain seemed to have kept both the good and the bad in their homes on this evening shift. Joseph cruised up and down freshly washed vacant streets with street lights shining globes accenting Brownstone entrances through the windshield's wipers dance.

The silence was broken as the Dispatcher put out a call for an Officer to respond to a call on Mt. Vernon Street, where an infant had stopped breathing. Revere flipped on his emergency red and blue roof flashing lights and sped quietly through the slick, empty streets in response. He arrived just minutes ahead of the EMTs and watched helplessly the volcanic grief erupting in the mother as her child was put into the ambulance. Officer Revere returned to his cruiser dug around in a pouch he carried on duty and retrieved a card with a number for a grief therapy group and gave it to the husband. There was nothing left there for him to do.

Now, back in the car, the thin rain seemed to become heavier, each drop pounding against the roof tapping out, 'zero, zilch, naught…life is not what you thought…' The waving windshield wipers whipping water now seemed to mock him. There was a throb in his temple and a shiver of pain in his heart. He headed toward Hancock Street with coffee and chili smothered baked sweet potatoes at Millie's Diner in mind.

He pulled into the parking lot and found a spot close to the front door. Through the picture window, like he was watching a drive-in movie he saw Jamie, the waitress, the real reason he frequented Millie's, racing towards a young female customer holding her throat choking. Joseph Warren raced out of his vehicle and through the door of the diner.

Jamie was now kneeling by the beautiful young woman who had turned a shade of blue. He pulled her up by the shoulders and applied the Heimlich maneuver to no avail. He laid her back down and began CPR. He listened for a heartbeat, checked for a pulse. He glanced over at Jamie. Thoughts of food erased from his mind. He got up and walked towards the door. "I'll call for the ambulance," he told Jamie.

While on the radio, Jamie walked out to the cruiser and handed Joseph Warren a large coffee. Then she walked to the front of the café under the awning, not wanting to go back in. The young cook came around the counter to take a look at the woman that had just passed, then walked out and leaned against the wall crying in the rain.

Joseph Warren was happy to see the EMTs arrive and when another cruiser showed up, he took the opportunity to leave the parking lot of Millie's Diner. His indigestion was acting up, and he still had not eaten.

He thought this shift was turning out to be a cruel joke. As a bachelor, what he thought about most often was a beautiful wife and a beautiful son. He had only responded to one call on this midnight ride yet would be filling out reports on two deaths before his shift was over. Everything felt heavier now. The bulletproof vest and holster belt with all it held weighed on him. The boots he wore were feeling like concrete blocks.

He contacted Dispatch again, and then he headed up Hancock Street toward the Old West Church. He decided to park in their parking lot and write up the two reports he would have to turn in before he ended his shift.

What should have been a peaceful quiet, felt more to Joseph Warren like an eerie calm. The asphalt of the parking lot glistened in the halo of the street lamps and the beckoning moon. Sheets of water rolled down the windshield obstructing his vision and a dog, far off, barked. Officer Revere finished writing his report, set the folder down on the seat, clutched at a burning in his chest and slumped over into darkness.

Nuelle pulled up Cambridge Street into the church parking lot. She and the carriage driver had had an unusually busy night. Her white mane weighed down with water clung to her side. Her tail waved, and ears twitched. The Carriage Driver was wrapped tight against the night. The sound of the wheels of the carriage echoed. Nuelle pulled the carriage a few feet from the police cruiser.

Officer Revere climbed out of the car and removed the holster and tossed it on the seat. He pulled out his shirttails and in a moment disposed of the bulky vest and put his shirt back on. The intense grip on his chest had been released. It took a moment for him to realize what had changed, but it had stopped raining.

When he was finally able to focus, he saw the carriage driver and Nuelle. He felt so safe. And for the first time in the longest time did not feel on guard and defensive. He walked over and gave Nuelle a pat on the shoulder. He felt an intense reverence for her, just like his ancestor Paul must have felt for his horse Brown Beauty. It was then that he saw in the carriage a beautiful woman holding a baby. In another moment, he recognized the woman from the diner and then assumed that the baby was the child from his first call of the evening.

In the parking lot of the Old West Church, first light shown on the alders in the parkway, no longer wrapped in the night's silence. The carriage driver stepped down and offered his hand in assistance into the carriage. Officer Revere, Joseph took his hand and climbed in, no longer weighed down.

"I am Joseph," he reached out his hand and smiled at the woman.

"I'm Sarah," she replied taking his hand.

Nuelle headed in the direction of Blossoms Street. She liked the route along the St. Charles in the misty morning hours. The couple in the back chatted away adding music to the ride.

Seventy-two hours later, Boston's finest turned out in mass at the Old West Church. A squad of twenty-one men wearing leggings, breeches, ash colored hunting shirts with billowing sleeves, with a powder horn draped over one shoulder and a pouch for musket-shot over the other shoulder stood waiting their order.

By command, the three rows of seven men made a show of loading their musket. The first row raised their muskets and fired. Then turned and formed to the rear as the second row fired and then also formed to the rear. The third row finished up with the twenty-one gun salute. The bursts of smoke left a whiff of black powder on the air.

There was tradition in Boston. There were old family lines going back to the very roots of the nation. The squad of Minutemen came to attention. They removed their three-cornered hats and held them by their sides.

While Boston slept, Ali Putnam was content to sit in her wheelchair and view her beloved Gouldian finches that she kept in the converted loft of her Brownstone. It was an expensive occupation with special flooring and lighting and heating requirements, but it is all she had remaining from her years tramping around the world with her husband.

She had left her seat on the board of the Natural History Museum at eighty when she was ordered by her doctor into the wheelchair to spare her heart. Old family money had saved her the task of working throughout her life but did nothing to prevent the pain of losing her family members one by one. Now, time blended and bowed as she sat and became lost in the sounds of the outdoors from exotic lands brought to her doorway.

She first thought of the idea of the aviary when the Museum Board voted to dispose of her husband's bird nest collection gathered from around the world on their expeditions. She had been boosted up many an Australian tree in her spry days, and those remained some of her happiest thoughts. The two of them would swim in warm lakes and make love in the grass. Their whirlwind romance had lasted for fifty-four years.

She kept other birds, but the Gouldian finches were her favorites. They were like flying rainbows she often thought and many a happy hour was spent this last decade with her imagining she was a bird, busy singing and hopping from spot to spot. She drew comfort from the idea of a nest and a close family chattering in the safety of their nest. Her heart leaped on the discovery of any new egg in a nest.

One evening a year ago, she sat quietly watching as first the tip of a beak, then a shoulder then a body cracked its way out of its shell, and a blue collared male Finch stood there inspecting his world. He stood out amongst all the rest, and she began calling him Murray.

It was no time at all before Murray found his roost on the wrist of Ali Putnam. Ali began talking to Murray to preserve the family stories.

Now, Murray was a capricious fellow who thought he could play hide and seek in the brush-wood from Ali. This caused Ali to laugh and laugh as his red head, and blue-collar were easy to spot even with the lush vegetation that had been established.

During the day, there would be a maintenance man or a veterinarian about. The men came to clean weekly, and there was even a gardener. That was during the day. At first, the evenings were for Ali; then it was Ali and Murray. Sure, she loved all the others. There were waxbills and spice finches and on occasion she would discover that a parrot finch had been brought into the population.

The aviary had become her world. While the household servants went about their schedules during the day, she slept. Her meals were made, and her servants served her. She filled her hours; her days were for sleeping, her nights – well her nights, were for music from the phonograph and providing for her flock.

Pure joy invaded her as she watched. She broke up many a quarrel with feuding factions and even had to scold a bird now and then for being too aggressive with one of her favorites. At one time she had banished one bird, she had to stay awake for the vet and as she rolled through the aviary pointing and chiding 'that one, that one right there' until he was caught and taken away.

This night, in her chair, she sat as conductor of her tropical savannah woodland. The wind section of her orchestra had joined in in harmony with the record playing. The parrot finches seemed to tap on their perches.

"Murray," she called, and he flew to her outstretched arm. "I feel like dancing," she smiled and rose to her feet her arm hooked as a perch. "Murray, when I go I want you to go with me. I hate to go alone. What if no one remembers me?"

Murray hopped along her glove covered wrist.

"We have been together for a long time now, right?" She turned as the music filled her. "I don't know what will become of you all once I go, and I don't want anything to happen to you. People can be so difficult."

Murray's head turned left and right. In Ali's eyes acknowledging that, he understood. She felt a bit dizzy from the turn in the dance.

She grabbed for her cane to steady herself. It was a beautiful Boston night with the sky littered with stars. Her eyes struck upon the window, and a sparkle flashed in her eyes. Murray fluttered to her shoulder. The phonograph was playing a sonata. Tears filled her eyes.

The window would not budge until she spotted the latch and turned it, and then it opened easily. The rush of fresh night air immediately got the attention of the members of the orchestra. First, one flew to the sill and cautiously looked through. It was soon joined by his mate and together they flew through the open window. The word went out, and more and more of her family fled into the Boston night. The phonograph played on. Ali would go and gently swing her cane at any who were still sitting in the woodland she created for them.

Murray hopped from shoulder to shoulder, not understanding why. Ali put the needle of the record back to the beginning. She walked to the window and saw her birds flying in all directions like rainbows coloring the night.

"Thank you, sir, for the dance," she said to Murray. "Why have you not flown away?"

It was when she slowly lowered herself back into her chair that Murray answered. "You asked me to go with you."

Ali Putnam stared at her friend. "Murray, I am afraid. I don't know how to die."

"Oh, Miss Ali, it is the easiest thing in the world. You will journey to where you have longed to go for so long now."

The Carriage Driver rose in the early hours. He went to the stalls and prepared Nuelle for their work of the day. Once they were ready, they made their way to one of their favorite spots and waited under the street lamp.

The Carriage Driver watched as many an unusually colored bird found perches in the trees and found grubs in the grass for food and raised their voices in the song that freedom brings.

There was great amusement in the Carriage Driver's eyes when a beautiful Gouldian finch with a yellow head and mauve breast landed on Nuelle's shoulder. Nuelle's ear twitched, and she waved her tail. After a moment, another Gouldian finch with a red head and blue collar arrived by the first. It was Murray. He bobbed about, ruffling his feathers to show off his colors. He fluffed out his forehead feathers. He spotted something on Nuelle's coat and pecked at it and shared his find with the yellow headed finch.

Nuelle began to pull away from the curb. Her head held just a bit higher than usual. This morning Murray sang, and did his best mating dance. The bells of the Old North Church rang out to wake the city to the new day.

Crystal rose early for this morning's run. She had been training for weeks now; logging forty miles a week in preparation. There was so much at stake for her; her personal confidence needed this. She had no thoughts of winning though it was an excellent fantasy winning the oversized prize purse. As a young mother, she felt she needed this boost, and this accomplishment would lift her.

She kissed her sleeping daughter on the forehead. "See you at the finish line," she whispered. She hopped into the shower for a quick rinse. She dried and put on her running shorts and white sleeveless shirt with a yellow stripe. Back in her bedroom she sat on the side of the bed and said, "Tom, I am going. I'll see you and Emmy at the finish line. She stood pulled on sweat pants and tied her pair of broken-in New Balance Zante.

She grabbed her bike and rode the few miles to East Main Street where the contestants gathered. It was a cool spring morning, and there was a sense of excitement and adventure in the air. She saw others pinning their numbers on and looked around for the check-in table. There was a large field running today, and people from all over the world had qualified and paid their entrance fees.

Crystal quietly thanked Tom again for giving her the entrance fee money as a birthday gift. She took deep breaths trying to store up oxygen. There were many people on the sidelines. The contestants walked around, some stretching their legs like ostriches, others waving their arms around needing to get as limber as possible. Some planned to carry a bottle of water some would rely on water from the wayside stations placed every mile.

The attendants were busy getting the contestants in the order they would begin the race. The ten o'clock hour was approaching, and that was the official starting time. It was a race; it was not a sprint – the pace would average eight minutes per mile.

A nervous man, number ninety-six, unexpectedly hugged her saying, "Good luck," and stood trying to shake nervousness out through his fingertips.

"Ready," came over a PA system. Then the starting gun was fired. En masse the wave of runners began. Crystal knew the pace was going to be rough at first and kept up. She never felt better. She even felt strong and confident as she passed by number ninety-six, then number one twenty-four. She was going to have to pick up her pace.

It was when Crystal reached Waverly Street that she reached her stride. She stopped seeing asphalt; her feet hit the long grass of the Serengeti, her hind legs became spotted as she transformed into a cheetah taking long, graceful strides. She made short work in passing the warthogs, Cape foxes, and the black-backed jackals. Then the bat-eared foxes and mongoose were left behind. She dashed by Roans and Puku alike. Now, in her vision she saw and overcame antelopes to her right and Masai giraffes to her left. Up ahead she spotted a young lioness on the heels of a wildebeest and raised her shoulders to make herself sleeker and passed both of them in the tall grass.

At Washington Street, there were waves of monkeys and gorillas off to the sides admiring Crystal's glistening coat. Her heart pounded out the rhythm along with her feet as she traversed the plains with the sun rising higher heading west.

The pack was thinning. The antelope and zebra were now behind her; the gazelles and wildebeests were to hunt another day. She was now amongst the strong and the mighty, the older trim cheetahs, the black leopards, and the muscular lions. There was still Commonwealth Ave to maneuver then Beacon Street.

The race was no longer against 25,000. The Savannah ahead was now filled with less than one hundred. She grabbed a cup of water as she passed a water station table and threw it in her mouth and let the water run out down her neck and onto her shirt. She swished what remained in her mouth and then spit.

Nearing Boylston Street she heard an explosion that tore through her Serengeti vision. The hunter's sting reached her as the debris of the blast tore her, pulling her to the ground like the clasping claws of a strong lion. She saw a black leopard knocked off his feet then right himself and stagger forward bloodied. From her prone position, she watched the horror on the faces in the crowds.

She watched as a calm white horse pulling a carriage stopped at the curb in her line of sight amongst the chaos that surrounded her. A crowd gathered around her body as she walked toward Nuelle. "Can you help me? Can you take me to the Family Meeting Area? I want to find my husband, Tom. He will be worried."

The carriage driver climbed down and offered his hand to Crystal. "Please climb in. There is a blanket there that you can warm yourself with."

"Please," Crystal asked again. "It is not far. Over on Berkeley and St. James."

"Sit back Miss. Nuelle and I will take you there first."

Nuelle had difficulty making any progress. There were thousands swarming the area. Emergency vehicles were coming in from all directions. Ambulances were carrying the injured to local hospitals.

As a child, Crystal had once sat and watched a rose open. It took hours for the petals to unfold. She was reminded of that now as she watched as the scenes around her unfolded in slow motion. There was no longer pain in her legs, and her lungs were not fighting for oxygen. The breeze cooled her, and she searched the crowd for the faces of Tom and Emmy. Her mother would be here by now.

Crystal could hardly wait to tell her mother how well she was doing in the race and let her sister in on her vision of running as a trim, powerful, cheetah through the tall grass overtaking impala and spotted hyenas with graceful strides.

As Nuelle pulled closer, Crystal spotted Tom holding her precious Emmy, and her mother was at his side. They were looking in all directions. Rumors and panic ran through the crowds, but Tom kept saying to her mother, "We said we would meet her here." Quietly he knew she should have arrived and he knew with an uneasy heart that nothing could keep her.

Nuelle pulled as close as possible. Crystal jumped down and ran to Tom. She hugged him and squeezed Emmy. She clasped her arms around her mother's neck and kissed her cheek. Tom felt the embrace. Emmy smiled at the caress on her cheek and tears formed in her mother's eyes.

The carriage driver stood by the steps to the carriage. Crystal knew it was time to go. She was wearing her best dress, and her hair felt like she had come from the beauty parlor. She had become aware of her surroundings in the sense that she knew she was no longer part of the chaos.

She sat tall like a queen in the back of her royal coach and thought about her day on the Serengeti.

Epilogue

This episode of The Carriage Driver is dedicated to Krystle Marie Campbell, who went out for a day of relaxation at the Boston Marathon in 2013 and lost her life.

The Carriage Driver - The Filmmaker

Nuelle always liked a light spring rain. Her coat glowed. She felt each raindrop grabbed some piece of grit from the Boston air and carried it to the resurgent sea. Today's rain was such, and she stood waiting at the curb free from worry or strain, breathing air infused by the sea.

The Carriage Driver's moleskin coat and hat glistened with captured raindrops, arrested from their path to the sea. He and Nuelle did not share the same opinion regarding rain. The work arrived whether there was a breeze or a gale. The leather top was put up, and the seats were dried, and they waited. He was a patient man.

Rain continued to drift down as the first of them arrived. The Carriage Driver referred to them as the Black Umbrellas. Now and then this happened. A handful came. They would be followed by more and more. They would stand in the rain swaying like waves in a tidal pool, and many kept a small candle burning.

Nuelle's pride was stroked as several from the crowd made their way to her and patted her shoulder; each one of them recalling their own ride.

Morris sat in the dark. The film he was working on was taking shape. A pile of notes had been made explaining to his friend in the cutting room that he wanted the long shots of the three-masted schooner left in, but they were not in the print and other matters.

His cigarette smoke curled as it cut through the flickering shadows. Many scenes changed, from pristine untamed African coastlines to towering buildings punctuating Manhattan. But his work in the shadows did not change. This dark room in the basement of his home did not change. He kidded himself that he may have spent as many hours in the shadows as all his audiences combined.

He remained unconvinced that he was an artist or had contributed anything original as his reviews announced. There were stacks of awards, but his soul questioned. He felt that too much smoke, too much alcohol, too little shaving and too few of life's pleasures were sure to be his legacy.

The bottle of Scotch beckoned him. Long ago, the clocks had been removed from the room. Time had no place in the dark. Here the eyes and ears floated above time. It was the whole idea of cinema.

Here in the dark, where eyes are bluer than morning. Here in the dark, a lover's kiss lingered, and all reframe softened. Here in the dark the lover's hands and the lover's cars hugged the curves.

He poured himself a drink, adding two ice cubes, swirled the mixture and downed the fluid. Then the very last frame of his celluloid life burned from the heat of the bulb. The loose, spinning film flapped with the clicking of the projector.

Nuelle waved her tail, and her ear twitched. The Carriage Driver sat straighter. The Black Umbrellas parted like Moses' sea, and Morris walked through the shadows toward Nuelle. He reached for a cigarette but forgot the pack on the table holding the projector. His lips were parched, and he wanted a drink.

The Carriage Driver climbed down and stood by the steps while looking into the faces beneath the black umbrellas and watched them weeping. Morris strolled, towards the carriage, a few hands were extended, and he shook them. He too looked into those faces of the unknown. Nuelle's white coat was centered in the frame of his mind, and he wondered if this was a Benzedrine dream.

As he reached the steps of the carriage, the Black Umbrellas folded closed, and drops of rain randomly extinguished the candles until the scene held only Nuelle, Morris, and the Carriage Driver. It was then Morris knew he was no longer the director.

"Step inside. There is a blanket for your legs to keep you warm." The Carriage Driver climbed up to his seat.

"I don't think I was done," Morris called up.

"You are standing here. The crowd has filed out. Climb in if you wish, you won't be disappointed." He waited.

Morris climbed in and seated himself. The red upholstered seat was the best theater seat ever. He grabbed the blanket and made himself comfortable. He looked around, "So, will you take me anywhere I want to go? Will you whisk me off to Mount Elikonas to the Temple of Zeus?" He patted his shirt pocket looking for his usual pack of smokes.

"We are more of an escort than a taxi," The Carriage Driver said over his shoulder. "You do have some options. You have earned that."

Nuelle was walking slowly along the St. Charles path. The Black Umbrellas lined both sides of the road. The effect of the candles dimming as they passed was not lost on Morris. He wished he had used it at least once in a film.

"Do you know who all these people are? I don't recognize a soul." Morris said to the Carriage Diver's back.

"They are people that you touched in some way. They are here paying their respects. By the look of some of them, by special request, they came back to be with you today. You made your mark, as they say."

The sound of the carriage wheels on the cobblestones reminded Morris of the sound of a projector. "So what are my options? I appreciate the ride, but I don't feel I was done."

"I tend to get in trouble with the boss when I give advice. I'll tell you what some people have chosen. A few become ghosts. They get a particular kick out of the idea that they were not done and needed just a little more time to complete loose ends. That is an option for you. Do you have someone you wish to haunt?" The Carriage Driver smiled, knowing from this man's movies that he did not want to remain on earth to scare anyone.

"No, that doesn't sound right though there are a few actors who deserve some spiritual maturing." He scooted a bit in his seat. "What else? I am not just going to sit around combing my wings. What about Atlantis, can you deliver me there?"

"There is something you might find to your liking." His hands, touching the reins, directed Nuelle to stop, which she did. He climbed down and went to the step and put his hand out invitingly to Morris.

"Is the ride over? Are you kicking me off?" Morris was tormented, finding himself in uncertain territory.

"No," replied the driver. But I think I have a solution for you.

"If I get off the carriage, can I get back on?" Morris asked.

"You have already earned your place. Your hunger has stilled. Nothing will change that now."

Morris stepped down. "So, what is the solution that you believe I will like?"

Taking a deep breath, he said, "You can do what you always have done. You can become a muse. There are creative people all around that could use a quick kick or a subtle prompt. There are artists and craftspeople that have these pent-up talents waiting for the slightest motivation. There are musicians that need to translate the music of the universe. And there is many a writer that needs to be warned about the dangers of adjectives."

Epilogue

An hour later Morris sat on the headboard behind Lois whose face was lit only by her laptop screen and whispered in her ear, "The Abandoned Libraries of Lost Cities," and then vanished from the room only to reappear at Harry's Bar and Grill. He sat on a bar stool next to a young man with shaggy hair and dangling cigarette with smoke curling into the dim light, nursing a half-finished beer and said, "Dead is a Long Time."

Morris was going to enjoy this.

When the members at the castle heard of his impending arrival, there were high expectations as they made ready his accommodations. Emissaries were sent in advance to study the surroundings this man created for himself in hopes of duplicating them.

The Flower Wind Tea House was crafted with attention given to every detail. The teakwood decks were always polished. The one hundred and forty-year-old oak sat in a porcelain container that measured fourteen inches wide and eighteen inches long. A bonsai master came in weekly to watch over the growth of his living forest. A stream built into the interior ran through three of the tea rooms. The banks were lined with moss and water trickled over the polished black river rock.

Hehuis Kanji's, Opera Cabaret was well attended. Guests arrived early for the limited seating event. They sat in small groups on pillows on the floor and experienced a tea ceremony from a Grand Master of the Urasenke Tea School. The barriers between people seemed penetrable during a tea ceremony. Pure enjoyment of friendship was obtainable. The ceremonies were both religious and spiritually cleansing.

Hehuis began his performance this evening from the empty wood-lined studio that served as a classroom during the day. It echoed his tenor voice throughout the Tea House. The songs tonight were created from poetry he composed and had been very well received. His slight build and poised features added to the calming surroundings.

At the end of the performance, there was much bowing in the tradition of the Japanese. When the guests were gone, he retired to a studio and while working on his last Ukiyo-e silence embraced him. Pictures of the floating world were embedded in his heart.

To his surprise, the body of Hehuis slumped before him. Hehuis walked through his tea house, his life's work, his temple, his tranquility. His students he viewed as disciples. His guests always left richer for their visits.

The heart floats free now
Above the world of sorrow
To his waiting arms

Two young Japanese women and two Japanese young men were attending to Nuelle's grooming. They bathed her. Two women stood on a crate and carefully combed, then braided her long elegant white mane. The men polished her hooves then brushed her coat and inspected her shoes. The Carriage Driver was quite amused at the proceedings. When Nuelle was finished, a garnish of color was added to the carriage.

The Carriage Driver went directly to the front curb at The Flower Wind Tea House. It was not the usual practice, as each arrival was unique.

Time passed like rain
In the forest of his life
Ringing bells follow

Hehuis shed a tear as he walked through the front door. He had haiku to write and had yet captured the grace of bamboo to his satisfaction in a watercolor. He went toward the carriage. The Carriage Driver stood by the steps. He bowed at the waist, then stood and extended his hand. Both men climbed onto the carriage. The peal from the bell of the Old West Church followed the single carriage procession.

Small sounds fill the gap
Left by your wings pushing air
Behind on your flight

Nuelle's hooves made clicking sounds against the cobblestones along the path to the castle. Her coat was powdered and perfumed; she was wearing someone else's vanity.

They soon arrived, and the large door opened. The Carriage Driver climbed down and helped Hehuis down. A tall, thin man wearing a tuxedo greeted him, and they walked inside.

What wonder is there
If nature is not waiting
In his Paradise

Once the word went out like ripples amongst those who had been honored to step inside the serenity of the Flower Wind Tea House they gathered. Some came to honor the singer, the writer of poems, the artist, some the teacher. Hehuis built his sanctuary and then invited everyone to join him.

The grand master of the tea ceremony worked his way to the front door, unlocked it and invited them inside. He began serving the last tea, asking those he served to be calm and respectful and allow others inside once finished.

Many drank their tea and on their way out paused momentarily one last time in the presence of the great bonsai forest. The students walked solemnly through the wood-lined room where they sat and learned from their gentle mentor. The grand master served tea until it was gone; he stood, bowed and left the building.

The Carriage Driver brought Nuelle to the stable. He removed the harness. He scrubbed the polish from her hooves. He brought two buckets of warm water into the stables and washed off the powder and perfume that had been applied to her coat. He then with patience and care took each braid down and brushed her hair, patting her on the shoulder now and then along the way. He cut an apple, and they shared it.

There is no winter
If others are by your fire
Embrace not the cold

Hehuis was shown into the main room with the every going fire. He looked at the walls of stone and the floor of stone. He was guided to a hard chair and invited to sit down. A woman dressed in white sat a plate of Ke-gani or horsehair crab before him brought in from the Hokkaido Prefecture. And another put down a white porcelain pot of tea.

Hehuis gently lifted the lid on the pot and saw a tea bag floating in boiled water. He sat the lid down, pushed the chair back and asked to be led to the kitchen. There was teaching to be done.

Allow time to slow
That you can accomplish much
And celebrate life

Once led to his quarters, he found a traditional setting, plus a workshop. On the counters were redwood seeds and acorns alongside empty ceramic containers. There were blank parchment scrolls and watercolors. He was pleased to find Koto and Biwa.

Just before the door was closed the usher said, "Your children have asked that you wait for them at the castle. They want to escort you the rest of the way."

Hehuis went to the counter and opened the bag of redwood seed and dropped them in water to prepare them for planting. He was in no hurry.

Epilogue

This story borrows from the life of Mr. Kaji Aso (1936-2006) He opened Boston's first Japanese Teahouse, "House of Flower Wind."

He was a poet, a painter, and teacher of Zen philosophy and in his spare time sang opera, performing his own opera cabaret, from his Fenway studio he also taught daily art classes.

I pronounce my fictional character's name, Hehuis, as He-who-is.

Do not blame him for the haiku found throughout the story. They are mine, and yes, they sound like fortune cookie messages. I know, I know.

No promises are made.
Make heaven here while you can.
The Carriage Driver

Professor Chester Langley lay cooling in his bed; his wife Mary kneeling by his side clutching his hand.

"Mary," Chester called, "have you seen my Walt Whitman?" He was busy stuffing a Mark Twain anthology into a small carpetbag. He looked around their room and the piles of books. "Mary?" He spotted a volume of Edgar Allen Poe and tucked that in the bag as well.

He went and sat on the bed near his wife. Her sorrow penetrated his senses. Today's event had not come as a surprise to him or Mary but was too dynamic an event for which to prepare. And now here he was. He leaned over and kissed her cheek tasting the essence of her in her tears.

He stood and walked to the bureau, opened the top drawer and took out two pipes. He thought to try and sneak them in wherever he was going. He tapped his coat pocket for assurance there was a pouch of tobacco and hoped it was allowed. He assured himself that a man's pleasures would not be denied.

He recalled his days as a freshman professor when he had met Mary. She remained his beautiful creature throughout their years. He spotted a small volume of Longfellow and slipped it into his jacket pocket. He scanned the books feeling remorse that there would be no room for Melville or Faulkner. A sigh escaped him when he realized that D.H. Lawrence and F. Scott Fitzgerald could only be carried in his memory.

"Mary, please take care of my Tennessee Williams and Henry Miller." Chester looked around. With a tear in his eye, he said, "And my Steinbeck." He spotted another small volume of

Byron that he knew to contain the poems, *Don Juan* and *She Walks in Beauty* and put it in his jacket's breast pocket.

Chester again went back to Mary's side by the bed. He took her hand, "Mary, if I am allowed to wait for you then I will. Look for me in an orchard. I think I can stand the separation if allowed the sanctuary of a tree to sit beneath and read."

He kissed his wife one last time and took his bag and went toward the door. He passed the Doctor and his daughter as they entered. He was relieved to see their daughter had arrived to comfort Mary. She looked so much like her mother.

Chester walked down the hall and front steps out into the night. He walked towards the Public Gardens he wanted to sit and gaze at the swan boats that he and Mary rowed without hurry around the lagoon during their courtship. He imagined Mary as his Princess Elsa and him as a knight of the Grail. *Oh, those happy years.*

Nuelle and the Carriage Driver waited patiently in the glow of the gaslight lamp while Chester made his trek towards them. The sounds from the Charles River garlanded the peaceful evening. Energy had returned to Chester's stride, and memories of him dashing towards his classes filled his mind. As he reached Charles Street he spotted the carriage; the carpetbag swung freely at his side as he approached.

The Carriage Driver seeing Chester approach, climbed down and offered his hand. Nuelle's ear twitched, and she wagged her tail. Once Chester was settled with his carpetbag by his side, Nuelle was given rein and paced slowly out of the lamplight.

The tranquil rhythm of the cobblestone's song relaxed Chester. He may have fallen asleep had not the spires of a castle appeared on his horizon. He absent-mindedly filled his pipe and lit it; he was afloat in fascination.

It was not long before Nuelle pulled to the front of the castle and stopped. A tall man wearing a tuxedo opened the double doors and walked toward the carriage while the Carriage Driver stepped down and assisted Chester. When Chester was on the ground, the Carriage Driver handed him a small package.

Taken aback, Chester sat down his carpetbag and opened it. Inside was a *The Barrack-Room Ballads* by Rudyard Kipling.

Once opened, the Carriage Driver said, "Everyone forgets Kipling." The two shook hands and parted. Nuelle made her slow turn back; happy in her work.

The man in the tuxedo indicated with his eyes and by clearing his throat that the pipe must be put out. Then the two entered. A chef from the kitchen peeked around the corner to see who had arrived, then ducked back to the kitchen.

Another man greeted Chester. "Let me take your coat sir," while putting out his hand. "Then I will seat you."

Chester was seated. He watched a smiling woman dressed in white walking towards him. She sat down a tray then placed a bowl of thick New England clam chowder in front of him. "Your fried clams will be out in a moment." She put a draft of Great Pumpkin Ale near his bowl and walked back towards the kitchen.

With a wide spoon of chowder in one hand and Kipling in the other, bliss engulfed Chester. It was a moment before he realized that a young man had seated himself across the table from him. Once refocused, Chester said, "Yes?"

"Sir, when you have eaten I will show you to your room. We have placed you near the back of the castle. It is a small but comfortable room. It is quiet, and as you requested it opens to the garden. A little orchard is there now for your use." The young man leaned forward and whispered, "You can indulge in your pipe while in your orchard." He smiled, stood and lifted the nearly empty glass and walked towards the kitchen, "I'll send out another with your clams."

In the morning, Chester opened two wide double doors and walked out to his orchard. It was a small orchard with about a dozen trees. He saw orange, pear, apple, and walnut. Vines decorated stone walls, and a flower bed surrounded a stone well. He walked around expecting to perhaps see fairies or gnomes. He did not spot any. He sat and leaned against a tree and began to read. As he read, flowers opened, and apple blossoms spread their petals.

Each morning he went out to his orchard and sat, often with his pipe in his mouth. Sometimes the pipe was lit but mostly it was just to assist in his contemplations. Day-after-day, he read to his garden. He watched the season's progress. He watched apples ripen and fall to the ground.

The pages of his books became worn and brittle. His Mark Twain had lost its binding. The leaves of Whitman were loose. He had memorized Byron and no longer needed to lift the volume. He could close his eyes and escape with Byron.

On the morning of his twentieth year, a bird landed at the highest point on the peak of the well. Chester paused and listened to the song. A young man came and sat beside him. "Sir, I have a story to tell you."

Chester sat up straight and listened.

"You have waited a long time. Through many seasons, you watched apple blossoms spread their petals and apples form and fall to the ground. It has been to everyone here's delight as each apple represented the birth of a child to a Boston family. Each child has grown to appreciate the love of words that you gave them. Each child has attended a university in your former community." The young man stood up. "I have a surprise for you." He waved his arm toward the doorway where Mary appeared.

"Mary! My Mary," Chester climbed to his feet rushing towards her. "Let me look at you."

Before him was Mary as she was in the days when they rowed the Swan boats in the lagoon on the Commons those many happy years.

The Carriage Driver – Ursa Major

Gary Beckman and Natalie Olson were born in the same minute, hour, day, and year, twenty-two years prior.

Gary stepped onto the bus in Oakland wearing his dress blues with his Seaman stripes on the sleeves and took a seat behind the driver. He was heading to Boston to keep a promise he had made to his former Petty Officer Second Class before his life was lost. Gary and the bus driver talked for the entire twelve hours of the first leg of Gary's journey. They would become life-long friends.

In Toledo, Ohio Natalie Olson stepped onto the bus. She took a seat near the front door. She and Gary Beckman talked for the last twelve hours of the trip to Boston. Three months later they married and became life-long friends.

Natalie could not decide which of their decades together she loved more, the first which was mostly making love, loud music, laughing and just getting by. Or the last which consisted of many a deep sea fishing trip and going to home games of their beloved Red Sox. Their fifty-two years together went by faster than a Rick Porcello fastball.

Now, the news brought home from his doctor's office was more than she could bear. He put on a strong face when he told her, but she could feel his pain. "Metastasized," he said with such a ring of finality. He told her he felt like he was deserting her.

Illuminated only by the light above the oven Natalie sat at her tile counter crushing, with a pestle and mortar bowl, pills found in their medicine chest. It was 2 a.m., and he could not sleep. He sat with pillows propped up against the headboard with a book he held but was not reading.

She put water in a pot and turned the gas on under it. When the water began to boil, she poured in the powder and stirred the mixture. She found the honey and put some into two cups. She then poured the mixture into the cups and dropped in tea bags.

With a tray, she carried both cups to their bedroom. "Here baby, I made us some tea. There is plenty of honey just the way you like it."

Gary took the cup and took a sip.

Natalie picked up a photo album she had placed on the nightstand earlier. She climbed into bed and opened the album. "Oh, do you remember that day? We had such a good time that day."

Gary stared at the pictures, his nerves unwinding. "You caught that big bass that day. I remember," he said smiling.

Natalie put her hand to his chest. She wanted to feel his heart beating. Lifting her cup she sipped. "There is plenty more, so drink up." She took another sip as did Gary. "Oh look," she said turning the page. "Remember this? It's the time you hooked that big tuna? I thought it was going to pull you over the side, and I latched onto the back of your pants with both hands. You did not know what to worry about more, losing that tuna or your pants. I still laugh about that like it was yesterday."

Gary smiled, "Sure, it wasn't you hanging out." He took a sip of the tea and had the first smile all day.

"Let me get you some more." Natalie returned with two full cups.

"What are you going to do?" Gary asked, holding back the flood inside him.

She kissed him on the cheek. "We have been through the rain and everything, and we are going to go through this together just like we have done all these years. Drink up. I am going to be with you every moment. It is you and me kiddo."

"The tea seems to be working. I am getting sleepy," Gary told Natalie as he scooted down and tucked his pillow under his head. A gray shroud moved towards him. But a moment later he felt Natalie as she curled up around him, put her hand on his heart and held him tight.

At Long Wharf, they boarded a schooner and sailed into Boston Harbor. The ship glided smoothly through the currents. The decks creaked as the sails were billowed by the wind. With Natalie at the helm and Gary by her side, they dined on fine salt air. The moon made the lapping waves look like fields of diamonds. She pointed the bow toward the constellation of Ursa Major, and they sailed away from the star-filled night towards dawn.

"Whales off the starboard," a voice bellowed from the rigging.

Gary went to the side to see a mother Humpback whale, that was longer than the schooner, and her calf. He then returned and took the wheel so Natalie could go and get a good look at the diving and emerging of the playful mascots.

"Let's go whale riding," she called and leaped onto the back of the mother whale.

Gary rushed to starboard. Seeing Natalie on the whale's back, he leaped over the side. He crawled up the whale's back and sat behind Natalie holding her around the waist.

The whale and the calf dived, and both Gary and Natalie found themselves witnessing the majesty of the sea from the viewpoint of the fish they had so often set out to catch. It was dark, but things looked amazingly clear to them.

Their eyes opened wide as the whales swam into a massive school of shrimp and began to feed. When done eating the two whales made their way back to the surface for air. Natalie and Gary sat on the back of the Humpback whale in the wild Atlantic.

She looked into the sky at the fading stars and took her last long deep breath. At that moment, she became a note in the song of the universe.

Gary stirred, and then was quiet. Gary Beckman and Natalie Olson-Beckman in the same minute, hour, day, and year sailed on.

Nuelle stood beneath the gaslight on Charles near Beacon St. Her ear twitched, and she swished her long white tail. She heard a couple laughing like children.

A few moments later a young couple came toward the carriage. They were leaning on each other, as young lovers do and whispering unheard words. It was a dry night, but both their heads of hair were wet and combed back.

The carriage driver could see stars in their eyes. He stepped down and said, 'Good evening. Climb on board. There is a blanket in the back you can use to keep warm."

Gary put out his hand, and the Carriage Driver helped him on board. He turned to Natalie and asked, "Are you coming?"

Once they were on board Nuelle was given rein to proceed. Natalie looked out into the sky and saw that they had a heading straight for Ursa Major.

Natalie scooted as close as possible to Gary and whispered in his ear, "I don't care what happens next." She put her hand on his heart.

The Carriage Driver – "Take Me Home"

His body casts a long shadow across the empty stage. Dust collected one by one on the seats of his auditorium as people, each stood in their turn and left him. Across the entrance doors of his existence, two surgeons now hung signs reading, *Performance Canceled.*

The evening sun came through the stained glass window splashing color onto the walls of the small hospital chapel. Upon feeling his absence, his Mother abruptly ended her prayer, stood and pulled her black shawl tightly about her face. She turned her back on the artifacts of the chapel and abandoned her book on the chapel floor.

His Mother returned to her bungalow and began making calls. She called his ex-wife and then his estranged daughter. She called his son in Alaska. She left a voice mail at his employers. One by one the prayers ended.

Nuelle stood attached to the carriage in the brackish night air beneath a flickering gaslight. She and the Carriage Driver had waited hours, as the man wrung his hands and paced next to them on the sidewalk. All the things he wished he had done were now going to be left undone. All the things he meant to say, but could not find the words were now lost. Piece by piece his life seemed to fall away as the audience ushered themselves to his exits.

The Carriage Driver stepped down when the man stopped pacing and put out his hand. When the last kind whisper reached the man's ear, he took the offered hand and climbed onto the carriage.

Nuelle's ear twitched, and her white tail swished as she was given rein. The sound of her hooves echoed the solitary song of the cobblestones along this lonely street. She walked past the castle without stopping. A short distance further a wide gate opened onto an estate, and Nuelle brought the carriage near the entrance.

The Carriage Driver climbed down and helped his passenger down and pointed toward the doorway.

The Rubenstein twins greeted him at the entrance. "We expected you hours ago," Jean said. "Little Annie is waiting for you out on the swings. You just have time to push her for ten minutes before we all eat."

He looked around getting his bearings.

"Where is my head? This way." She clutched at his arm and guided him out the back where children were playing.

He saw the little girl on the swing and walked towards her. Upon seeing him, she screeched with glee, as little girls do.

Danny, a boy about five, looked up when he heard Annie. Upon seeing him, he ran towards him. "Am I the first to say hello?" Danny asked. "We have the boat ready. Can you take me out on the lake in the morning? You can teach me how to fish, Ok?"

He knelt down and received a hug. "Sure, I look forward to it." He stood and walked up to Annie.

She jumped from the swing and gave him a hug. Then she jumped back onto the swing. "Push me before they call dinner. Please."

He began to help Annie gain some height on the swing, but not too much height, as he looked around. The small lake was wooded as far as the eye could see. He spotted a young man and young woman swimming near the dock.

"Dinner!" Susan, Jean's twin sister called.

Annie hopped from the swing and put out her hand for him to hold. "Come on; I'll show you the way."

Danny walked at his other side.

A place was set at the head of the table for him. Susan showed him to his seat.

He looked at the long table filling up fast. He was introduced to Dave, a man a few years younger. Then for a moment he wondered what age meant now. Jean sat to his right.

"Did Danny already ask you to take him fishing? I am afraid he was very anxious for you to arrive. The rods are already in the skiff. Did you see it?"

"I did," he nodded taking it all in.

"The others are dawdling," Jean said. "Do you mind coming with me?" She said to him. "A couple of them are in the artist's room. You can come help me drag them to the table."

They walked through large double doors then up some stairs, then into a hall lined with windows overlooking a lighted tennis court. Jean walked into the artist's room, "Come on guys. He's here." He stepped into the room behind her.

One man put down his brush in a can of linseed oil so it would not dry. The other set down a sculpting knife that he was using to shave clay from a bust of a distinguished lady. "I am Christopher," said the sculptor.

After wiping paint from his hand, the man who had been working on the oil painting put out his hand and said, "James. Has Danny already seen you? I'd like to go with you two."

"Sure," he said. "What time should we get started?"

"Not too early. Danny will get tired after a couple of hours, and there is choir at 11 a.m." James walked toward the door while Jean was still smiling.

When James, Christopher, and Michael were in the hall ahead of Jean, they heard her say, "I am going to stick my head into the writer's room and see if Margaret is going to join us this evening. You guys go ahead."

Through the window, Michael saw a game of doubles going on at the tennis court. He heard music coming from somewhere in the house.

Back at the table, the food had arrived. Susan was serving Annie, and Danny waited patiently as his food had been served.

Margaret and Jean found places at the table. Dave and James sat talking.

"Michael, will you lead us in grace this evening?" Jean asked. He noticed she winked at him.

He watched Annie put her hand out to Danny. Then Jean took Annie's other side, and James took Danny's. The table became quiet.

Michael looked at his plate that was no longer empty. "Our hearts are now full in your presence. May our family grow ever closer, infused with love and tenderness as all pain is surpassed, all addictions expired and all memories of wrongs forgotten. We who were broken are now healed. We, who were alone on our stage, now sing to a full house. Our laughter will echo in the halls and decorate the woodlands. Here every kindness is returned, and our table is blessed." Michael looked across the table at Danny and said, "Here where, in the morning, Danny is going to catch his first fish, Amen."

There was a quiet chorus of, "Amen."

When they were finished eating, Christopher stood first and picked up his plate, then Danny and Annie's. "Danny, run up and get your and Annie's bath started. Margaret will be up to help in a minute."

Jean and Susan started clearing plates. Michael stood, took his plate and an empty bowl that had held rolls and headed toward the kitchen. Dave stood by the sink with the hot water running. James stood by with a towel to dry.

Outside the teens who were swimming and playing tennis were now eating around a campfire.

Jean called to Michael, "Are you too tired or can you read Annie to sleep this evening?"

Michael smiled.

"In my Father's garden, I pulled weeds," the man said leaning forward talking to the side of the Carriage Driver's head. "He ran a nursery, and just like the shoemaker's son who had no shoes, I was not there for flowers but as his servant. On Sunday's the people came. We did not open officially until 8 a.m., but he and I were always there early. There were busy people; they wanted to gather their flowers and plant early. He would oblige them, collect the money and I would load the flowers into their cars after putting down some paper on the floorboards. Many of the customers were women. They always showed their appreciation for Father, much more so than the men. The women would often give me a small tip for loading their purchases; some would pat me on the shoulder, I liked that. Of course, I was always made to hand over the tip money to Father. 'For a rainy day,' he would say counting it out, and handing back one-quarter of it." The man sat back. "I guess I am talking too much."

"Go on," said the Carriage Driver. Nuelle liked the timbre of the man's voice; it reminded her of the voice of the Carriage Driver.

"There was one woman, her name was Mrs. Green. I thought she was pretty in her blue jeans, sneakers and white blouse. She wore a headband to keep her hair off her face. She always had a pair of gardening gloves hanging from her back jean's pocket. She and Father would talk flowers while she gathered her selections. She admired Gardenias and Rhododendron and brought them to her sunroom. Father was with her every step of the way through the garden.

There were hanging plants all along the rows of slatted wooden benches that Father and I built. Their fresh pine tone was long faded from wear and water, and they now sported a rustic hue. The Fuchsia suspended their purple-blue teardrops catching the eyes of every passerby from their mossy cradles. If Father were nearby when someone stopped by the bird-of-paradise plants, he would tell them pointing at the spade-shaped leaves that, 'This is an off-shoot of plants at the Royal Botanic Gardens.' That sentence would often have me lugging a big plant to their car." The man adjusted himself in his seat.

"Oh, I have a story for you, in the heat of the day, I was to ride my bike down to the dairy and load a trailer that was left there with manure. Then after work Father would drive the pickup over and hook the trailer up and bring it out behind the nursery and the manure would be used in our planting sheds. I got paid three dollars by the Dairyman for that, and I got to keep it. Yes, that happened almost every week during spring and summer. That gave me spending money all through the summer. Of course, I mostly worked, so there was not much time to spend it."

The Carriage Driver noticed that Nuelle's pace had slowed and recognized that she was enjoying the passenger's stories.

In the afternoons, the workmen would arrive. They would load bags of mulch and other amendments into their trucks. They did not bother me with loading. I would get the hose and give all that needed one a drink of water to cool them off and make their leaves shine. It was the quiet time of day under the shade of the suspended black mesh. Father would often go out and pay suppliers and make a deposit at the bank. Since there were few, if any customers in the afternoon, I was left in charge. Any workmen would just sign for what they took, and the bill sent to their employers." The man gazed out across the Commons, thinking about those early days.

The Carriage Driver heard him sigh.

"One day a rickety old rusted out pickup pulled to the back of the nursery hauling a trailer. It was loaded with scraggly looking plants in old worn out busted up wooden box planters. Some of the boxes were tied together with rope. The driver climbed down and went and found Father. They talked a while. Father handed over some money and the driver, and I pulled those old splintered boxes off his trailer. It was tough work, and I was drenched in sweat when finished. The old man barely broke a sweat. He wiped his hands then shook my hand and drove off leaving the mess for me. When Father arrived to see if I had finished, I asked him what we were going to do with these.

He said, "They are yucca, we are going to put them in new wooden boxes with fresh soil with good drainage, we are going to trim all the dead sword-shaped leaves, just leaving the crowns and you are not going to believe the beauty of them when they are properly cared for. You and I are going to care for them. They can survive the worst neglect, but they will thrive with care and attention. Don't you worry they will not be here long, their first large burst of panicles and they will find new homes. At that point, he spotted a hearty woman carrying two large coleus plants one clutched in each arm; smiling he smacked me on the shoulder and told me to get started, and then rushed to her aid. With his big hands, he scooped them out of her arms, bringing a glowing smile on her face as they walked laughing to the counter."

"Well, I pulled those boxes under the shade of a jacaranda and listened to the woody seed pods tap out a calypso against the stone wall along the back while filling new planters and grooming the plants to their purpose. There was a natural beauty to their thorny crowns. Father saw those plants for what they would be."

The man paused, and the Carriage Driver looked over his shoulder at him. He saw a sad expression form.

"When I was fixing to graduate high school my Father became ill. Shortly, he was gone. When going through the house cleaning up his belongings I came across a locked metal box with my name painted on it. I broke the lock on it, out of curiosity and found a letter and some bank passbooks. I won't tell you all the letter said, 'cause it broke down like this. It said the Dairyman paid ten dollars a trailer load to have manure hauled away. He paid me three of it and gave the seven to Father when he brought the trailer back. The bank books showed weekly deposits which represented my pay, tips, and the manure money. That money went a long way towards my education. At the bottom of the letter, it was signed 'A Rainy Day, Love Father.'"

"After I finished school, a job brought me to Boston, where I worked and lived. I raised my family. I took good care of them, the best I could, they never went hungry, and we saw to it that the children wore clean clothes. Maybe not the best clothes, but always mended properly. Each in their turn grew and went on their way. Each one was nurtured, getting enough sun and enough nourishment. Then each seemed to transplant themselves to other parts of the country. Well, I hope they do not take as long as I did in discovering the simple beauty of life. It took me years to figure out that my role there was less important than being there."

The Carriage Driver – Man in the Dark

Club Grotto's stage was small and dark with only one spotlight on the man in the center. He wore brown slacks, long sleeved white shirt, and suspenders. His polished shoes were brown with a white vamp. His wise face was brown with a white dusting of beard. His forehead glistened. The silver saxophone bounced light into the darkness of the club. Curling smoke traced the outlines of moving silhouettes and empty wooden chairs. Gerald Brown, the man on stage, blew air through the hollow caverns of his sax and stirred souls.

Gerald Brown was born blind. He had no rainbows. But because he was blind, he was never restricted by vision. With the aid of his silver horn, he turned air into magic. In the hallowed air - fear, depression, and loneliness were driven out of the club. Those who bathed in his music felt cradled in safety. The music came from deep within him and stirred passions – couples danced slowly.

Club Grotto closed at three a.m. The patrons moved slowly out into the night, back to their incomplete lives. Gerald packed his saxophone carefully away and made his final exit into the shadow-filled alley.

Nuelle stood beneath two gas lights that cast a glow upon her the carriage and the Carriage Driver. In the distance, they heard a tapping. Gerald made his way to the carriage; red tipped cane lightly tapping the street. When he reached them, the Carriage Driver stepped down and said, "Welcome," as he reached for the man's hand. "One step up," he said, as he guided him into the backseat.

"My God," escaped from Gerald's mouth.

"Yes, indeed," the Carriage Driver responded.

The first man Gerald ever saw was the Carriage Driver, Nuelle, the first horse. The light from the gas lamps made him stare. He was greeted by stars and moon. The mixture of sounds and sight overwhelmed him. The cobblestoned path before him brought tears to his eyes. Leaves on swaying tree branches performed their ballet. A Homeric laughter bellowed from the backseat.

Nuelle pulled from the curb. The wheels rattled along the cobblestones. The Carriage Driver sat straight and was amused as Nuelle led them first down one street then another. She then turned up toward the park, then along a path of the St. Charles. She was slow and deliberate. She went passed gazebos trellised with honeysuckle and down a street with clothes billowing on a clothes line. The tour continued to the surprise of the Carriage Driver. Then he was overcome with understanding as Nuelle went to his and her favorite spot looking out towards Graves Light. He realized that Nuelle wanted her passenger to see his first dawn.

The Atlantic did not disappoint as the arms of daylight spread across the blue-black water and broke the grey-domed sky. A trolley lulled its way into the bay and a sailboat glided across the silky sea. Gerald leaned forward, "Do you hear that?" He called towards the Carriage Driver.

"I hear the call of the waves and the greetings of the seagulls," was the reply.

Gerald was barely big enough to contain his smile.

Nuelle backed up a few paces and returned to the cobblestone streets heading towards the castle in the sky. Her gait was paced evenly; they were in no hurry as Gerald's face kept moving in all directions. His eyes widened at the sight of the castle. He gripped the saxophone at his side to help with the anticipation.

Nuelle stopped in front, and the Carriage Driver stepped down and held out his hand to assist his passenger out of the carriage. The wide wooden front doors opened, and a tall man wearing a tuxedo walked toward them and greeted Gerald.

He was brought to a table. "Sir, you can leave your horn on that chair while you are served."

A woman wearing a white linen dress down to her ankles walked into the room carrying a tray. She held one-hundred percent of Gerald's attention. She sat a plate of Sicilian Sautéed Chicken simmered in Marsala in front of him. Next to that she sat a small plate of Amaretti. The label on the wine bottle read Patelin de Tablas Rosé. The small print said, *Gigondas.* Once she poured him a glass, she said, "Save room for dessert, Pere Ripiene alla Milanese will be served when you are ready."

Her voice was like honey; he had spent years recreating the mood with his saxophone that she created so casually. He sighed when she disappeared through the door. His food was perfection and the wine soft. As he contemplated his good fortune, another woman took a seat across from him. She also was dressed in white. A significant difference and something he had trouble dissolving were her wings.

"I am one of the many who will welcome you. I won't say we were waiting for you," she paused. "One never knows."

Gerald did not appreciate the diction and felt her pauses were a bit overemphasized. He took a sip of wine and then another bite of his meal.

"Don't feel you have to respond right this minute. You just arrived. We understand that you were given the gift of darkness at birth. You did such a remarkable job with darkness; we thought you might consider another gift."

Gerald did not like where this was going and wished she would just say whatever it was she was trying to say. He resorted to another sip of wine. Then he popped an *Amaretti* into his mouth, glanced at the door, and wondered if he should make a break for it. He wondered if the horse and carriage were still outside, or if he'd have to walk back. The first woman, the one who had served him came back through the door, walked to the table and put one hand on his shoulder and with the other filled his glass. Her smile settled him down, and her friendly wink made him forget the idea of escape.

The woman in white with wings began again, "We had a meeting, and we feel you would be perfect for the job. Gabriel is doing it now but has asked for a change."

Gerald took another sip of wine.

"You might want to take it easy with that; you know, first impressions and all," her smile was reassuring.

"Do all angels fidget and hem and haw?" Gerald asked.

At that moment, a gentleman of about Gerald's age came into the room. Gerald found it interesting that the gentleman was carrying a trumpet that had been fully engraved with *art-deco* patterns. Without waiting to be asked, he took a seat at the table. "You might want to listen, it is a good offer; it is an offer that does not come around too often. Heck, just sitting where you are sitting is an offer that does not come around that often."

The gentleman put his hand on the shoulder of the angel. "I have a good feeling about this. You were there with him this morning; he heard it. Present the idea. If he doesn't like it, there will be something else for him."

The angel with the white wings made a funny little face, "Like I was trying to explain, Gabriel has had this job for quite some time now and has asked for leave. Your work has inspired so many now, and you have always worked the night shift and well; this is really big; we are offering you the job of heralding in the dawn."

Gerald's eyes lit the room.

The Carriage Driver – Spirit Jumping

The Carriage Driver stood in darkness, shoulder to shoulder with Nuelle, looking out over the slumbering Atlantic towards Graves Light. There would be no work for them in the morning. The carriage, leather upholstery glistening, carpets brushed, brass polished, would remain parked. His weathered profile reflected in Nuelle's eye by the burning embers in his ancient briarwood pipe.

It was at midday in the Commons when he first noticed the young boy of about twelve. He was wearing his cotton newsboy cap backward on his head. From cloth sacks, over his shoulders, he was posting bills onto trees. He was a blue-eyed boy, wearing pants that ended at his calves. It seemed to the Carriage Driver that the boy was one hundred years out of place, which made him a curiosity.

The Carriage Driver climbed down from the carriage and walked the thirty yards to the last tree which a bill was posted. He reached it and tore the poster down and held it in his hands. It read, 'Spirit Jumping' and had tomorrow's date. He walked back to the carriage and sat the poster on the seat beside him.

Jennie lay in her ICU bed and peered passed the locked arms of her prayer circle that blocked her every possible escape. Beyond the human barricade, she could see the Commons, and she connived to gain access. She could see women pulling along little children, one in each hand. She saw a few old men in wheelchairs along the pathways. Her vision was somewhat obscured by the barrier, but she also saw young men and woman waiting in anticipation.

Unseen by her prayer circle, bubbles floated from the core of Jennie. Bubbles filled with her excess hope and helpfulness breached the circle. Capsules laden with temperament and discipline floated towards the Commons. The stream of frothy air was added to by James in surgery. His vital signs waned as shells carrying passion and patience drifted away from him, towards those gathering in need of what they felt missing.

Mothers with their children gathered in hopes of rounding out gaps in their existence. Old men staked out their positions hoping for the slightest respect and tolerance. Young women seeking kindness and love and loyalty stood waiting for their chance. Angry men stood tensed ready to grab their share of contentment. Young girls sat on the lawns with their skirts neatly tucked beneath their knees in anticipation of an additional dose of modesty.

An automobile calamity sent the driver's assertiveness and confidence tumbling toward the Commons as more people arrived having read the posted bills. The car's passenger added beauty and caring for the treasures showering towards the Commons.

The atmosphere was electric. A vain of absolution prevailed. Both the good and the bad were made available. Morgan passed by his own hand when he saw on his computer screen his carefully planned deception was discovered; pellets of his greed and recklessness bounced through the Commons alongside released anger, from an untouched woman.

Aging grandmothers, with posted bills clutched in their hands, conspired to pass along as much compassion and confidence to their granddaughters that they could carry. Men of ill will and ill health arrived escaping their destinies, releasing lust and jealousy amongst those gathered.

At dawn an exalting rain began; the tumbling, floating, drifting, bubbles, shells, and pellets pelted, leaped and saturated the seekers that had arrived early to fill their cup of life. Mother's tears were hidden. Young boys found doses of courage and integrity. Young girls skipped away filled with purpose and graciousness. The old men soaked in their wheelchairs rolled themselves away with peace and honor in their hearts with their lots in life. Grandmothers in weakened capacity knelt and kissed their rosaries as they watched their granddaughters graced with unbeknownst joyfulness.

The keepers of records in all directions made note of those passed on the day of spirit jumping. All penance today discharged and all exaltations freely forfeited. Those baptized with rain scampered from the park graced with what others left behind and that for which they'd yearned. The believers dispersed stronger and prouder, with new knowledge of the bounty of life. If what was offered was accepted it was carried away; the pain seeped back into the earth captured and stored for another time.

Jennie's prayer circle wept, believing they failed. The surgeon tending James fell back on his training that he was going to lose patients during his term of practice. The authorities carried away Morgan's body wondering how people could behave so badly. The ambulance attendants at the scene of the auto accident shook their heads and thought what a waste of two young lives. Young, old, good and bad, all contributed.

The Carriage Driver stood next to Nuelle in her stall and brushed her coat. This was not the first time they were idle. There were many days without passengers. But like weathered New England fisherman, they went out in the mornings, doing their jobs. Today was different. He stroked her with the brush with the strap over the knuckles. It was one of those mornings when the rain steamed off the pavement after it fell. He talked quietly to Nuelle. He confided in her, and she listened. They had been together a long time.

When he finished brushing her, he slipped her bridle on and walked out into the sunshine leading her. He wanted to go to one of their favorite spots. In fact, it was the spot where they stood in the gloom of the night before. In the sunlight, Graves Light was undetectable. It was a long walk, but they needed to be together. It would be a long day for them. The Carriage Driver felt alone, and there would be no passengers to guide until at least the morning. “In the morning, first thing we are going to the Commons and tearing down every bill posted on every tree. Then things will get back to normal,” he patted Nuelle’s shoulder and fed her a half an apple.

Nuelle swished her tail and rustled her mane. “Yes, you are right,” the Carriage Driver agreed. Their passage was closed. The thought entered his mind, today the many portholes to perdition were also blocked by bills posted on a termite infested boards in the ground. The signs read, ‘Closed - Spirit Jumping’ and they had tomorrow's date on them.

The Carriage Driver – The Devil's Tail

It was the Fourth of July. At the sound of the popping noises, Madeline set down the fan blender paint brush she was holding and walked away from her easel, towards the window. From her third floor window, she expected to see fireworks. But there on Ruthven Street two rival gangs were fighting their own revolution. There were so many of them that it gave her a fright. Roxbury was not always like this, but now, street turf wars were commonplace.

She knew better than to stand at the window, but the sound of approaching sirens and flashing lights added a surreal soundtrack to the chaotic scene below, and she could not step away. As her eyes followed the characters on the street, the sky began to fill with bursting color from across the river. Cascades of glittering phosphorus now darted through the skies before reaching their final crescendo. As if on cue, the lighting director lit the stage.

The last sound Madeline heard was the breaking of her window pane. Her easel stood guard over her and down the hall a tea kettle whistled.

Back at the window, her gaze widened as first one then another small black metal buggy arrived on the scene each pulled by a small black horse. Little men dressed in uniformed black climbed down from their seats. Their uniforms included handsome black boots, and each carried silver tipped black canes. The distance played tricks on Madeline's eyes; if asked she would have been forced to swear that tails were draped over their shoulders.

The men in black escorted two of the men that had been lying on the ground to their separate carriages and scurried away into the earth. Crimson flowers continued to bloom in the sky with great fanfare. Two police vehicles arrived, sirens blaring, and the officers joined in the bizarre ballet on the stage before Madeline.

A flurry of black transports with dapperly dressed men arrived pulled by glistening black horses to escort the fallen. The black shuttles were arriving from two directions with practiced efficiency to collect their fares. One driver climbed down and waited, he stooped over, pushing his red face, close to a man on the grounds face, staring into his eyes, letting him know what the next moments would bring. The man's last act was to scream.

Madeline's thoughts were torn between the coaches that whisked this way and that and the tears of the incendiary flowers that drifted aimlessly toward darkness. They were soon followed by a kaleidoscope of newborn color.

Two more, white with blue striped police cruisers arrived. One officer was down, and a man in black escorted him to a waiting coach.

Nuelle, the white mare was guided by the Carriage Driver. They arrived at the curb on Ruthven Street in front of Madeline's building, to the consternation of many of the dapperly dressed men in their handsome boots. They felt this was their turf.

As Madeline approached the carriage, the Carriage Driver climbed down and extended his hand to her. "One step up," he offered.

A little man in black made a hasty approach; his tail dragging behind him. "What's this?" He demanded, "This is my fare." He tapped his cane on the walk in an authoritative manner.

The Carriage Driver turned to him and smiled. Madeline took the Carriage Driver's hand and stepped up into the protection of the carriage. The Carriage Driver said, "Do you think you have the ability to take her from my carriage? In a snap, I can have an army by my side. Will those in your custody come to your aid?" Two more pairs of red eyes stared in their direction. At the same time, Nuelle took two steps backward and the wheel of the carriage accidently pinned the man's tail to the ground. Nuelle's ear twitched, and her mane swished in the air.

The eyes of the well-dressed man bulged in their sockets, and his face which was already quite red turned redder. "You did that on purpose," he yelled at the Carriage Driver, who stepped up to his seat and took the reins.

"Make yourself comfortable. There is a blanket if you feel the need for one near your feet."

As Nuelle pulled away from the curb, more police cruisers arrived. The black fleet scattered into the night looking for more fares. The remaining players disappeared into shadows; stage trap doors swallowed them, and the curtain came down. The ballet was complete, and some of the remaining troupe was escorted away bathed in a red and blue hue of the cruiser's lights against the faded brick, dirty windows, and darkened hopes on Ruthven Street.

The driver with the damaged ego and smashed tail climbed back into his empty shuttle and drove off the stage of the ballet. He tucked his tail into the epaulet at his shoulder; rushing off he kept a close eye out for future passengers. The night was young, and there were always ample fools.

Madeline sat back in her seat. "You know it was not always like this. But just like watching a tree die things went bad. First, a few leaves wither and fall to the ground for no apparent reason. Then you'd look, and a branch is bare. That brings the bugs, you know termites and beetles. Before you know it there are holes bored through and through. The tree fights and fights. Someone comes along with a saw and takes the limb down. They finds nest inside where lots a damage that was not seen before is now exposed. Then pretty soon what was green turns brown-gray as the life escapes it. Well, that is what is happening here on Ruthven Street. Seems the bugs got down into the roots and just choked the life out of it. Guess there is nothing can be done."

She paused, but the Carriage Driver knew she was not finished.

"Most of the decent people were driven out. The small merchants, those that could not afford to pay for security were driven out by extortionists and thieves. Those that did not go just got older and older as the brown-gray set in. Guess that means they also got out, one way or another." She leaned forward, "Where did all those black buggy's come from? Where were they going? I never seen noth'n like them before. Have you? Those little men are something I am not going to forget soon. But you know what? I was not scared. You made it, so I had nothing to be scared of. Most of my life I have been scared. But not tonight, no sir."

There were still some scattered fireworks decorating the sky. Nuelle pranced slowly allowing her passenger time to enjoy them. She made her way down towards the gardens of the Commons along the river. Muted laughter from those enjoying their holiday floated over the river. In one direction, she could hear someone singing, and he was accompanied by a dog barking from another direction. Madeline thought the air was different here. The air seemed unspoiled here something she was unfamiliar with. The glow of the fireworks aided by the gas-lit lamps along this passageway brought a fairy tale charm to the surroundings of the carriage. Madeline pretended it was all for her.

The Carriage Driver smiled, "You will never be scared again. All memories of hunger and sickness will soon be gone. All your pain has been left at Ruthven Street."

The Carriage Driver - The Master's Wine

Stackjack Jack is what the boys at Bedford Textile Mills called the old man who maintained the looms. Jack worked at the 'Mill' for twenty-seven years and was looking forward to retirement. The news of the plant closing and that the pension money was gone through bankruptcy proceedings did not go down well with him.

He first went to the library and found some required information. Then he went to the bank for enough money for a case of good wine. When he had done what he intended and got confirmation the wine was delivered he drank his own medicine. His passing did not make it into the newspapers.

When her husband died in a military conflict, Elsa took work as a domestic. She and her young son shared two rooms and a bathroom in the sub-quarters of the Beacon Hill estate. She had been told that there would be a dinner party this evening which meant working very late. Her task would be to serve and to clear. While in the busy kitchen, Elsa answered a knock at the back door. A delivery man stood there with his clipboard for a signature with a case of wine at his feet. She signed, lifted the box and set it on a counter where the steward would see it.

The guests started arriving after eight. The kitchen staff was busy preparing the meal as the couples arrived in their beautiful automobiles wearing evening clothes for the occasion. The guests were seated at a long table. Before them was bone China, crystal goblets and silver utensils with their maker's markings. There were three couples on each side of the table and the host, of course, sat at the head of the table.

The steward removed the candelabra from the table. Then he walked to the kitchen. He was surprised to see the case of wine but did not question it. He opened two bottles and put them on a tray to carry to the table. Every detail had been attended to, down to the size of the linen napkins. Elsa and another domestic waited before they began to serve. When the steward was finished pouring the wine, John Powers stood to begin his toast.

"Ladies and Gentlemen," a broad smile filled his face. "We are the *nouveau riche* or lace curtain Irish, as we are sometimes referred." The females at the table giggled. "Seven months ago we took control of Bedford Textile Mills, five months ago we shifted the pension funds and three months ago we declared bankruptcy. The Federal prosecutors have been faced down by our lawyers. The last of the workers have been laid off and we at H.I.T. Capital have pocketed forty-two million dollars for our efforts." John Powers lifted his glass of wine. "To the masters of the universe, long may we thrive."

Each drank to the toast. The steward was around quickly to refill the glasses. Elsa began to serve one side of the table, and the other was served by the second girl, who was hired for the evening. There was clam soup, and salad then leg of lamb and local cranberries, there was abundance and laughter. The jewelry sparkled, and the men looked forward to Cuban cigars. The wine flowed.

The steward and two servers worked quickly, quietly and efficiently. They took care of the guests every need. Once the meal was finished and dessert savored, the group took to a nearby den. Clean wine glasses waited and were continually filled.

Elsa cleared the plates and glasses, and the helper began gathering the silver to be thoroughly cleaned, polished and stored. In the kitchen, Elsa combined what remained from the wine glasses on the table into one glass and drank it down.

At about midnight, the lightest of the guests, a woman in a white gown slumped over, palms up, to laughter from the others. Shortly a second guest buckled over. This time, no one laughed, and her husband rushed her to his car and headed towards a hospital. He died at the wheel of his car. Ambulances were called by the steward as more guests, and John Powers crumpled to the floor.

The emergency staff at the hospital had a busy night with poison control. Four of the twelve guests did not make it. The rest were hospitalized. Police were notified and went to the home of John Powers.

They began their investigation. After questioning, the steward directed them to Elsa's quarters where she lay holding her young son. The boy was taken into child protective services.

Elsa's spirit rose. She did not want to leave wearing a gray dress, white nurse's shoes, and white apron, so she found her floral print dress and slipped into it. She put on casual sandals then sat at a mirror and took her hair down from the tight twist that work required. She found a small satchel and put a few things inside. She looked around the room that had sustained her for the last two years. She spotted her son's teddy bear and picked it up. Clutching it to her breasts, she left the house. She felt calm and without burden.

Nuelle was not too familiar with Beacon Hill area, having little reason to frequent its streets. The white mare did like the first days of autumn after the lingering Indian summer. The streets were clean, and the air was refreshing and still.

Elsa stepped out of the large double doors onto the porch of the house and walked down the steps to the sidewalk. It was a beautiful New England morning. It was quaint. She looked at a beautiful white horse pulling a polished carriage. She took the scene in and turned and walked down the street. There were flags waving in the breeze. The gentle wind tossed her hair and hem of her dress. She had not felt like this since before her husband's deployment. She thought for a second about coffee at an outside café but was not carrying any money.

The Carriage Driver was quite amused. Nuelle made no effort to overtake Elsa. She matched Elsa's pace and let the morning take its course. Elsa stopped she felt that the carriage was following her. She turned and walked toward them. He stopped the carriage and climbed down extending his hand. "One step up," he said. Nuelle swished her tail and twitched her ear. "Your husband is waiting for you." That made Elsa's heart soar.

She turned, put her arm on the back of the seat, and looked back, thinking about her son. She held tight to the teddy bear.

Nuelle's hooves sounded out a melodic cadence as she made her way to the castle. She pulled close to the front doors, and a tall man wearing a tuxedo came out to greet her.

The Carriage Driver stepped down and put out his hand. Elsa stepped down with her satchel and the bear. Her eyes opened wide with wonder.

She was led inside. There at the single table in the room sat her husband. Upon seeing her, he stood and rushed to her. Once the greeting was over, they were both seated back at the table.

Their first meal together was of New England clam chowder and seafood. A woman wearing white arrived at the table and into the two silver chalices sitting there she poured the Master's wine.

Footnote:

The tabloids were having some fun with the terrible news, some of the headlines read, Boston Herald Muscatel Murders, The Boston Globe, It Doesn't Always Pay to be an H.I.T. Man and the National Enquirer ran, Board of Directors gets Stiffed.

Tori sat on the hope chest at the end of her bed and prayed tightly. Her pink fingers confirmed the seriousness of her need. "Momma always told me that moms would be there when you needed them the most. Well, my Momma is in trouble, bad hospital trouble and needs her Momma. Can anyone hear me? I don't know her name; I just called her Nonna. We just have pictures of her now, if you need one to find her. She had a nice smile and always gave me a firm hug. You gotta send Nonna soon. Oh please."

It was a busy night for prayers. Christians all over the Middle East were praying they would return home safely from their conflicts. Christians all over the West were praying that their loved ones would return home safe from the vigilantes that roamed the streets of their various towns, cities, and states. In every borough, village, hamlet and ghetto people felt that good had been defeated and now the cardinal sins were waging war with one another. Gluttony seemed to prevail.

Tori's prayer ascended, it bumped its way upward, looking for space and guidance through the maze of prayers. Then a soldier in the Somalian dark stopped firing his rifle at silhouette figures and the shapes stopped firing back. Tori's prayer slipped through the space left in the mass of prayers. A phone rang in Topeka, and it was a job offer. Tori's prayer soon filled that sliver of space, pushing ever higher.

St. Maria Goretti supervised the staff attending to children's prayers this evening. The prayers were being sorted into piles, from the least expedient to the most urgent. It seemed a typical night. There were lots of requests for a bicycle from young boys. Others asked that their parents stopped screaming at each other. The girls mostly wanted phones and permission to wear makeup.

Tommy Griffin was on staff; he had drowned in 1864 trying to save his sister from the Mississippi River. His sister sat next to him. When Tori's prayer arrived, it was Tommy who received it. He pushed back in his chair toppling it. That was a surprise and shocked St. Maria Goretti. He rushed forward and recited it to her.

St. Maria Goretti was the right person for the job, being both saint to children and grandparents. *Why do they all have to be named, Nonna, Mimi, Gammy, and Nanny?* She smiled to herself. There was work to do.

The Carriage Driver did not question things he was directed to do. He had been around too long for that. He readied the carriage and guided Nuelle into the harness. He made his way toward the castle without a passenger. He pulled up front and went inside to see if there were further instructions.

St. Maria Goretti was having some trouble. She felt that it should not take any time at all to locate members of her flock when needed. Nonna was found working on a mosaic in the great hall. She spent day and night there among the innocent artisans. When she received the word, she set down the chip of red tile that was to be placed amongst the depiction of the Final Victory that adorned the hall.

Valencia Bishop, Tori's Nonna, asked, "What on earth?" Not expecting an answer.

'Precisely,' St. Maria Goretti thought. "This way. Tommy and Mary Griffin offered to glide you to the castle. Your granddaughter is asking for you."

The words hit Val hard, and she hurried along the hall with St. Maria floating behind her. Tommy and Mary were waiting. When Val reached them, each gently took an elbow, and she was lifted and floated effortlessly back towards earth.

The Carriage Driver had only waited a moment when they arrived. Val was brought to the step of the carriage and waited for a hand up. Tommy leaned over and whispered in his sister's ear. "Let's go with her."

Mary smiled, and the three settled into the back of the carriage.

Nuelle made her way easily and sure footed. She stopped directly in front of Tuft Medical. The Carriage Driver stepped down and assisted Val from the carriage. He then turned waiting to help Tommy and Mary.

"Sir, take us to this address if you would. We want to see the little girl whose unselfish prayer is being answered today. Then I fear you will be required back here." Tommy's cherub face beamed grace while Mary's displayed porcelain angelic beauty.

When all were on board, Nuelle was given her rein and although she was given the signal to turn left, she pulled right onto Harrison to the amazement of the Carriage Driver. Nuelle glanced over her shoulder and turned right onto Berkeley then left onto Washington. It was obvious to the Carriage Driver that Nuelle had something up her sleeve, but he did not know what.

It was then that Mary yelled, "Stop." She whispered into Tommy's ear and pointed. Somehow they had arrived in front of a pet store.

Tommy and Mary jumped down and ran inside. The Carriage Driver climbed down and pulled an apple from his pocket. He cut the apple into quarters and fed two pieces to Nuelle and two he ate himself.

They waited about ten minutes when Tommy came running back, "He wants money. Do you have any?"

The Carriage Driver laughed and emptied his pockets and handed Tommy what money he had.

Tommy ran back in, and in another ten minutes had traded the money and one miracle, to the teenage clerk, for a three-month-old Retriever named Picasso. Tommy, Mary, and Picasso climbed up into the carriage, and Nuelle proceeded to the address indicated to the Carriage Driver.

Tori's Father Mark had just set the receiver down with the bad news from the hospital when he heard a knock at the door. He picked up Tori and they walked toward the door.

Seeing the dog, Tori wiggled out of her father's arms and gave this beautiful dog a hug that would bond them forever. Mark looked this way and that, but only noticed a carriage being pulled by a white horse.

He bent down and patted the puppy. He patted Tori and said, "Don't strangle her." There was a receipt clipped to the dog's collar.

Tommy and Mary were whispering in the back of the carriage. Nuelle's paced slowed. "Stop," Mary called. The two children jumped down from the carriage. "We are going to go back and be her guardian angels. Will you tell Val for us?"

"I'll meet you there. You can tell her yourself."

Mark got their new family member taken care of with water and some food. He took Tori and buckled her in the car. They headed to Tuft Medical to say goodbye. Tommy sat on one side of Tori and Mary on the other. They were holding her hands.

Arriving at Tuft Medical, Mark found a parking space in the front. Feeling crushed, he climbed out of the car and spotted a carriage with a white mare parked in front. It puzzled him. Holding onto Tori, he walked towards it.

Once there, Tori pulled away and leaped into the carriage. Val and her daughter Victoria sat there. Val looked at Tommy and Mary and understood they were not returning with her. Mark stepped inside and gave Victoria a farewell hug and stepped down. Val held Victoria's hand. Tori gave the biggest hug to both of them, clasped her hands together in prayer and said, "Oh, thank you."

With tears in her eyes, Tori put her foot on the carriage step and climbed into her father's waiting arms. Picasso waited. There was work to do.

At the services, a speaker relayed to the weeping guests the story of how Tony received his nickname Apollo when stepping out of the shower below decks on the U.S.S. Enterprise that was floating in the South China Sea, off the coast of Vietnam. John was stoned. Paint it Black by The Rolling Stones was blaring through the bulkheads and the boredom. Finishing up, former Seaman Eddie Roscoe cleared his throat, holding back tears, "That was forty-three years ago. Today we mix their ashes for eternity."

Michael, Tony's brother, stood next and walked to the podium, he cleared his throat. "I am always the last to know, or understand." It was an admission of guilt. "It was not until John passed those years ago now, that I understood how much Tony loved him." He looked out over the crowd through bleary eyes. "They have mixed Tony's and John's ashes and those ashes, for now, rest on the hearth. But will be brought to Brisbane per their wishes. But to me…" He took a deep breath.

"This is how I see it….

At the moment of Apollo's passing, he was met by John. Now, John was in the back of a golden chariot pulled by a beautiful white horse. Of course, John was wearing a Hawaiian shirt, and broadies, tan legs sported feet clad with huaraches sandals. He wore sunglasses and beamed a smile as bright as any lighthouse. There were cases of Boag's Draught at his feet and their winged Pegasus readied for a trip to the Coral Sea and the Great Barrier Reef.

The party had been going on for a decade now. Large fifty-five-gallon drums were cut lengthwise and now were filled with charcoal and a metal grate held endless quantities of seafood and steaks were sizzling. Girls danced on the sand to the same sounds played on beaches all over the world. A trio of calypso gypsies pounded on their steel drums as clouds on sand danced about their feet.

There were shirtless senoritas and handsome young men with dreadlocks. There were bohemians and bakers, mavericks and meter-maids, and waifs and wayfarers. There were clusters of people sitting by the tree-lines and wisps of white smoke rose from their circles into the sphere of colorful low hanging Japanese lanterns.

The village beyond the treeline sat at the foot of a waterfall cascading into a deep pool. Women wore grass skirts, and the roofs of the huts were gifts from the palms. The air was decorated with the songs of tree dwellers. A hand full of guinea fowl and pheasant pecked at the ground between huts.

The golden chariot landed with practiced grace. John hopped out and unloaded the cases of beer as Apollo took it all in. Pegasus lifted off to shouts of 'hurray' from the crowd. Apollo yanked off his shirt and headed into the warm crystal blue water. John went splashing into the surf after him."

Michael paused. He had lost his audience. They found themselves among those on the beach. Their earthly worries momentarily suspended as their hearts were carried away to carefree sand and surf. Apollo had a way about him. His priorities were not conventional. He was not raised in the world of nine to five. He did his duty, but then his life was his own. He walked among the living but did not seem to witness much living. He built fish ponds and filled walls floor to ceiling with aquariums until they came alive. His curious eyes seemed to see and recognize everything and his smile was permanent. His friends clung to his spirit on this day. His presence buoyed them in life, and now today, he again lifts their spirit. His body was gone, but his warmth remained.

One by one the audience had mentally joined in at the beach, shedding their 'Sunday best' that convention prescribed. The woman now wore bikini bottoms, and a flowery silk wrap draped over them, the men were barefooted and wore gnarly barracuda trunks. Some now had deep sea lines cast into the surf; some were sitting in the shade of a palm tree talking peacefully to a fellow traveler. There were pineapples and mangos and laughter.

The boredom of war brought together Apollo and John as did the sea. Now after a lifetime of bonding and a period of waiting they once again found themselves.

Now, in the warm water of the Coral Sea, they swam. As they swam, two curious white sharks streaked towards them. The fins of the sharks were easy to spot as the wave began to form. Each man started to swim quickly towards the shore when the sharks came up fast, and just like Navy Seals using centrifugal force to be pulled into a motorized life raft, they each caught a fin and pulled themselves onto the backs of the sharks, they stood and rode them along the surf and to the shore.

A line of shapely hula dancers had formed and not ones to pass up on the fun, Tony and John joined in. The very palm fronds above them swayed in rhythm with the hips of the Gidget instructing. The boys swung their hips and wiggled their fingers, this direction and that until they could not stand it anymore and fell to the sand where notes of music swarmed about them like bees and laughter rode the sunlight. As they lay in the sand, John rolled to his side and said, "Let's go up to the village. I'll show you our home."

Michael looked out over the crowd, "Well, that is the way I see it." And he stepped away from the podium.

It was a cool evening in Boston. The fog had rolled in on Beacon Street. The Carriage Driver stood by Nuelle. His carriage was spotless and the rigging shining. He reached into his pocket and cut an apple into quarters. He fed two to Nuelle and ate two pieces himself. The gas lamps illuminated the scene as they waited. "I guess some people are just not ready for heaven," the carriage driver said to Nuelle.

The Carriage Driver - Camera Obscura

Paulino Gray was a simple soul. At forty-five he held a job in the back workshop of The Salvation Army on Massachusetts Ave. He was one of those souls that had no knowledge of guile, cunning, or deceit. And because of that many thought him slow. When his parents abandoned him, his uncle took him in.

His uncle Alonso collected cameras, and Paulino knew that if he brought home any odd, old looking camera, he would be showered with joy and happiness and maybe ice cream. Over the years, there were many joyous occasions between this cobbled together family.

Paulino was confused when news arrived at the workshop for him to get to Lemuel Shattuck Hospital quickly, his uncle was very ill. Paulino walked in circles trying to gather himself. Then he with great effort pulled himself together and proceeded to the hospital. Paulino spent several helpless hours at the bedside of his uncle. He was then told with regrets that his uncle had passed. His soul being soft and gullible had no protection from such pain.

In the following two weeks, Alonso's estate was settled; a lawyer arrived and had Paulino sign a few checks to pay up some outstanding debts at the butchers and the bakers. The house that they lived in now belonged to Paulino, who was alone.

Just when things were getting back to normal, Paulino heard a knock on the front door. The caller caught him just as he was going to do the dishes and was surprised when Paulino opened the front door wearing an apron. "Sorry, to disturb you at home Mr. Gray, but your uncle passed away owing me one thousand dollars, and I am here to get a check. Just make it out to Cash."

Paulino was confused, but then he pulled himself together, he found the checkbook and wrote out the check. The man thanked him with a wicked smile and rushed off to the bank. Paulino went back to the kitchen to finish up his chore.

After the kitchen was straightened up, Paulino went and sat in his uncle's den. There were bookshelves protecting books on cameras and photography and photographers. There was a taxidermy stuffed black bird. There were photos of Alonso's wife who passed long before he lived there. There were a dusty globe and a Tiffany lamp. He sat in his uncle's cracked overstuffed leather chair. He scanned the shelves filled with cameras, many of which he had bought from his employer though he had to admit some were donated to him with a smile. It was then he saw an envelope leaning up against one of the cameras on the shelf. He stood and picked up the envelope and stared at his name printed there.

He carried it back to the desk and stared at it a long time, wondering how a letter got there. He was told his uncle was gone, yet here was an envelope with his uncle's handwriting on it. He put his palms of his hands on his forehead and stared at the envelope. Finally, he sat up straight with determination and opened it. It read:

My poor sweet Paulino, you have been given the gift of innocence. It can be considered a cruel gift, but that is not the way I see it. I am sorry that I no longer can protect you. Many years ago you brought home this camera. I found it to be quite unique as it only projects the truth. Many times I viewed you through it and was filled with joy. Now, you use it to find happiness.

Your loving uncle,

Alonso

Paulino set the letter down and tried to think what it meant. He stood up and went to the camera that the letter leaned against and lifted it from its dusty shrine. In the dark room, he shifted it this way and that; he clicked the shutter; he raised the viewer to his eye and scanned the room. The aperture caught what light there was and brought visions to him unseen in his history. He pointed the camera at the globe and found the African continent and its horrific cinematic history began to play. He lowered the camera and looked around the room, his eyes rested on the black bird, and he lifted the camera which projected this crow picking the bones of a dead fish found on a polluted shore.

This fascinated Paulino. He found an old leather strap and made clips and attached the strap to the camera and hung the camera around his neck.

He went to work wearing the camera around his neck, and many of the others made fun of him. After work, he went home. Just as supper was ready, there was a knock at the door. A serious looking man stood there. He began to speak, and as he did, Paulino lifted the camera and pointed it straight at the man's smiling face. Dark withdrawn pools replaced his deceiving lying eyes and spindly carbon veins crisscrossed through his temples, cheeks, and nose and he wore centipedes for a mustache. Paulino dropped the camera, which was caught by the strap and screamed, "Go away," and then he tried to quiet his heart as he slammed the front door in the man's face.

Paulino paced and wrung his hands and paced some more. He was not a child, yet he had never seen such things. He went back to his uncle's den and read the letter again, 'use it to find happiness' was the message. He could pass through this new found adit as the aperture opened all that was hidden.

Mostly the camera scared Paulino; he began using it only outside where there were both air and room to run if need be. On a Saturday morning in the Commons, he sat on a bench and people watched through the camera. Some appeared as weasels, some raccoons, even precocious monkeys; there were those that seemed to have retained innocence, but they were mostly young children.

He continued his walk looking at people with his camera; then he turned the camera on a woman his age sitting on a bench with a bag of bird seed in her hand; birds happily feeding at her feet. Her reel played a life of gentleness, kindness, and affection. Life had wounded her, yet, here before him was a person, both bright and talented, both loving yet shy. He made up his mind to muster his courage and go over and introduce himself.

Patience watched as this man approached her bench. He was slow and deliberate, with an old camera dangling from his neck. She mostly noticed that the birds did not fly away. They did not become agitated to any danger. She was still contemplating the birds when he sat down beside her and said hello.

Down the lane, Nuelle swished her tail and twitched her ear. The Carriage driver sat patiently with his passenger named Alonso in the back. It was a gentle New England morning. Birds accented the air and children laughed as they played leapfrog, another group played red rover and ran about enjoying the park.

Something made Paulino lift the camera towards Nuelle and the carriage. What was projected made his heart glow. A golden passageway loomed before his eyes and there in the back of the carriage was his beloved Uncle Alonso waving good-bye. To the Carriage Driver Alonso said, “We can go now.”

The Carriage Driver – Life of Your Time

The old clockmaker sat in the Commons and stared up into an old Washington Elm with its winter branches flowing like tributaries of an ancient river back into the thirsty sky. There was a gray dampness in the air, and the clockmaker wondered what part he played in time. He remembered back to when he wanted to be a botanist but was stirred into apprenticeship to the Howard Clock Co. by his father. And now he had spent his life in the business of time.

The Carriage Driver sat tall, a shawl around his shoulders, hat to keep the dampness off his head and watched as people gathered near his carriage. Some claimed to have earned passage, yet, none had. He watched the old man on the bench looking up into the elm and waited patiently for him to make up his mind. Nuelle was comfortable and enjoyed the evening air. The smell of smoke from the Carriage Driver's pipe lingered.

Konstantin drew his gaze from the elm and looked around at the hustle and bustle of people as if powered by their own mainsprings. The thought of their spiral torsion spring of metal ribbon, inside them with measured release of the tension intrigued him. There were many differences in their outer appearance, just like clocks or watches, but their inner movements were surprisingly similar. Wound just to the right tension they each, slowly release their energy throughout the life of their time.

Konstantin thought about how many elegant grandfather clocks he had opened up. It was often a cold and solitary pursuit. He dusted and cleaned them, replaced worn gears and applied fresh lubricant to the bits and pieces that made up the workings. It did not go unnoticed that what clockmakers had been doing for hundreds of years, to extend the life of clocks, now the medical profession had taken up.

He looked back into the elm and saw how high it had reached and in how many directions it had extended its arms. No doubt arms raised in praise to all that was above waiting, yet with its roots clinging to this earth. He thought of this three-hundred-year-old elm, which only needed night and day to survive. Then he thought back when there were no clockmakers, the only measurement needed was the sun hitting the horizon and the day was miracle enough for all. Time began when people exclaimed night followed day and it was then people began to feel the need for hours, minutes and then seconds. Once seconds arrived, the sun hitting the horizon ceased being a miracle.

The Carriage Driver carried no watch. He went about his task when and as needed. He, like Nuelle, liked all the people they meet. He climbed down, took an apple from his pocket and cut it into quarters; he fed two to Nuelle and ate the other two himself. He watched the passersby and wondered if he would ever meet them.

Nuelle swished her tail and twitched her ear as the old clockmaker stood. To the sounds of thunder, Konstantin set his gold pocket watch down on the bench, having no further need of it. He looked around and spotted a beautiful white mare and walked towards her.

The Carriage Driver tapped out his pipe and waited. Konstantin arrived smiling, "I think this is where I am supposed to be; can you give me a lift?"

"Do you know where you want to go?" The Carriage Driver asked in a confiding voice.

"Can you bring me to the land before time?"

Nuelle swished her tail and twitched her ear as the Carriage Driver assisted Konstantin into the carriage. Nuelle seemed only to take a few steps until they were in a large open area with a few trees. To his right was a field of larch with their needles turning a brilliant yellow. The air carried the yap of river otters, and white-tailed deer paused in curiosity. Varieties of orchid, lily, goldenrod, and aster vied for his attention. There kneeling beside a freshly dug hole was a beautiful Indian princess.

"I think this is where you are meant to be," said the Carriage Driver as he stepped down and extended his hand to assist Konstantin. When his foot hit the Earth, he found that his hands were no longer knotted and the pain in his knees was gone. He has back in the body he'd grown accustomed to at age twenty-five. His eyesight was keen and sharp. His hair brown and shoulder length. He was once again filled with the vigor of youth. He felt charged with the air breathed by Mariners.

To Konstantin, even Nuelle's coat looked brighter, and the Carriage Driver's shoulders seemed broader. He turned and gazed at the woman.

"This is Raaina, she is part of the Massachusett tribe, and this is her land, she has been waiting for you."

Konstantin looked at the Carriage Driver and back to the woman who was ready to plant an elm that a few moments ago he may have sat beneath looking skyward. She stood and walked towards him putting her hand on his heart. "You and I are going to make a timeless landmark that people will come and enjoy for a hundred generations. This will be our labor and our joy."

The words rang like a song in Konstantin's ears. Raaina rolled out a bark with the area laid out. If measured it would cover fifty acres. Pathways were scratched in, and the area included a small body of water near what would someday be named the Charles River. There were many tiny trees near them, their roots bundled tightly. Konstantin was in awe of the beauty of the expansive uncluttered land; in his ears the spellbinding sound of the not too distant vast restless Atlantic; he felt he could breathe in the whole canopy of sky and exhale the universe.

The Carriage Driver having delivered his fare climbed on board, he looked around with a certain envy at the sight of this new world, then guided Nuelle back through to where they came from. They returned on a rainy Boston evening and made their way to their favorite spot beneath two gaslights that illuminated the path to the carriage.

Raaina and Konstantin began their happy toil. They both knelt and planted the Washington elm seedling. There were no more thoughts of seconds or minutes. The concept of hours faded and soon there was no need for Fridays or Mondays. Seasons sufficed. They made trips together to the far north and brought back different trees for use in their grand endeavor. They both fished and bathed in the river. Birds filled the skies. They were both filled with the joy of sunrise and sunset brought them moon glow. Soon their son arrived at their longhouse.

The Carriage Driver sat tall, thinking of the land before time where there was no need for clocks. In the distance, he spotted two tiny silhouettes walking along slowly, making their way towards the carriage. Nuelle sensed their approach; she was pushing thoughts of the land before time from her mind.

Footnote:

I found it interesting while doing research for this story that the Catholic Church has no saints for time. But Saint Eligius of Noyon is the saint of clock makers and carriage makers and horses. I just could not seem to fit him into the story.

Around the middle of the story when trying to find a way out, I thought E.R. Burroughs had written about the land before time, but instead, he wrote, *The Land That Time Forgot* (1918) Edgar Rice Burroughs.

The Carriage Driver – Johnny the Dime

Nuelle pulled out onto the quiet streets of Boston in the gray hours of Sunday morning. She had not gone far when a carriage wheel hit a pothole and cracked. The Carriage Driver, who had been jolted through and through climbed down, turning his back this way and that; he bent down to inspect the damage. He stood and walked to Nuelle and said, "Hey, girl, we have to go back." He then walked to the rear and putting his back into it lifted the wheel from the rut. He called "OK" and began to push as Nuelle pulled. She knew the way home.

Reverend O'Leary of Cathedral of the Holy Cross quietly went about his business preparing for mass. He felt the sermon would move his flock this morning. It was his day to relay the word to his parishioners. He had just greeted the organist, and the altar boys were changing from their street clothes.

People wandered in. They sat or knelt and while waiting quietly prayed. The pews slowly began to fill as the beginning of mass approached. With a few minutes to go before it was time for the Reverend to approach the podium, 'Johnny The Dime's' black Cadillac pulled in front of the church, and he and two bodyguards climbed out and went inside.

Johnny the Dime tapped his finger into the holy water and dabbed his forehead; he then walked near the front and took his seat. Two women at the end of the row got up and moved elsewhere to make room.

As the Reverend began, Johnny the Dime grabbed his chest, and his case was closed. At the same moment, two small black metal buggies arrived at the entrance of the church. Little men dressed in black uniforms climbed down and approached the doors. The first reached for the handle, then lowered his hand then reached again, but his arm was frozen. He tapped his handsome black boots and clicked his silver tipped black cane on the ground. The little man next to him was bolder. He grabbed the handle of the church entrance and traded his hand for his courage.

Inside the church, those in attendance spread like ripples in a pond away from the body. The sun that had been streaming through the arching stained glass windows filled with gloom. A flurry of black transports with dapperly dressed men arrived pulled by glistening black horses. They were now watching each entrance.

The Reverend phoned for an ambulance. People slowly moved towards the exits but were held inside by lurking darkness. Word had gotten out about Johnny the Dime, a news van arrived, and a crowd began to form. Two police cruisers showed up and nervously began crowd control. The very air surrounding the church was now charged with prickly, Goosebumps trepidation.

A rookie cop began to write a ticket for one of the little black buggies, but a sergeant came over and whispered to him, and he put his ticket book away. The little men dressed in black cast giant shadows along the pathways. The rookie turned to the sergeant and asked, "Why did they call him Johnny the Dime?"

"He broke all the commandments is the reason I heard, and looks like he got away clean with it all."

An ambulance arrived. The paramedics rushed in with their gurney and lifted Johnny the Dime's body unto it. When they reached the door, a dark looming shadow rose from him.

For a moment the little men in black stood back, but then first one then another, then another grabbed hold of the spirit of Johnny the Dime and wrestled it to a waiting black transport as the bodyguards stood by helpless. Sun once again filtered through the stained glass windows.

A side exit door opened, and parishioners rushed out like bees escaping a hive.

A block away near Mystic St. in the back lot of the Salvation Army, a teen tossed her newborn that she had wrapped in yesterday's newspaper in a dumpster.

The Carriage Driver had just lowered the jack and tested the weight of the new wheel when he heard Nuelle's call. He quickly put her into her harnessing.

She cantered up Brookline and then onto Washington. On Mystic she slowed, then pulled next to a fence along the back lot and stopped. The Carriage Driver climbed down and walked up to Nuelle while looking around. Nuelle nudged him and pulled as close to the fence as possible.

The siren of an ambulance cut through the air. Nuelle bit at the fence with her teeth until the Carriage Driver climbed up onto the carriage and dropped over the chain link. He looked around but did not see anything. This made Nuelle agitated, and she pounded her hoof on the ground and against the fence.

The only thing near them was a row of dumpsters and bails of clothing. He lifted one lid and reached inside. He stirred things around and found nothing. He lifted a second and by chance a small arm appeared from some newspaper that unwound when he stirred. While balancing the lid of the dumpster on his head, with some effort he was able to reach inside and bring the child into his arms.

With the child in his arms, he walked back to the fence. He could not climb it holding the baby. He laid the child on the asphalt and with his foot he pushed the chain link until there was just enough room to slide the child underneath. Then he huffed as he climbed back to the carriage.

Sweating he picked up the child and climbed back on board. Nuelle twitched her ear and waved her tail and shook her head. She pulled away from the fence along an alleyway towards Mystic St. She turned toward Washington, and the carriage's left wheel hit a pothole. The jar went straight up the Carriage Driver's spine, and Nuelle thought he let out a yelp.

In a moment, the yelp turned into a hysterical, full lung complaint about life in general from a little passenger in the arms of the Carriage Driver.

Nuelle turned off Washington St. onto Monsignor Reynolds Way, which passed in front of Cathedral of the Holy Cross. The crowd had thinned out. A patrol car was still there. A police sergeant, bodyguard, and a little man in black were standing together smoking. Other little men wearing black uniforms, were about to pull from the curb then stopped and stared as The Carriage Driver went by. Nuelle walked proudly, chest out. She turned onto Dedham St. and pulled to the curb in front of Wediko Children's Services.

He climbed down and made his way to the front door. After pounding on the front door for a couple of minutes, he realized it was Sunday, and it was likely closed. Just as he stepped away, the door opened.

A woman with crystal blue eyes looked at the Carriage Driver, then at the wiggling bundle in his arms. "Why, what do we have here?" She reached out and took the child.

"He is a gift from the universe and needs someone to look out for him for a short period of time. Do you think you can find someone to watch over him?"

The woman stopped her humming to the boy. "We have people waiting. I am sure we can place him in a warm home."

The Carriage Driver thanked her and turned to walk away.

"Wait, does he have a name?"

The Carriage Driver smiled and said, "Call him, Johnny O."

It was the worst of times. Belle grieved both aloud and quietly over the years about her youngest son Todd, who was reported as missing (M.I.A.) in Afghanistan in 1985. Daniel, her husband of 53 years, passed away two years prior. There may have been best of times, but they were now forgotten by Colt and Mariah.

Now, Colt Matherly sat in a chair by his mother's bedside. On the other side of the bed sat his sister Mariah. Her mother was looking at Mariah with a blank look on her face, no recognition.

"Mom," Colt said softly but got no response. "Belle," he said trying her name.

She turned her face towards him. He was not used to the lack of recognition, but he had managed to hold back his tears. He picked up her hand and gripped it firmly.

Belle turned to him. In her face was the aura that he recalled from his childhood. He could feel her grip tighten on his hand. He reached across the bed, and Mariah took his other hand. The trio formed a triangle of sorts. It was just the three of them now. He stared into her eyes. He looked through her eyes.

Colt was first to find himself in a forest by a lake. His mother was lying on a blanket. Mariah was sitting with the youngest, Todd, playing some kind of hand slapping rhyming game. Colt looked towards the lake where his dad had a fishing line in the water. It was sunny, but the trees knocked fifteen degrees from the temperature by the water.

Colt, who had a beach ball by his side, lifted it and threw it towards his mother who managed, to not catch it, but stop it. She picked it up and stood. She ran toward Colt and hit him with the ball calling, "You're it." Then she dashed away. Colt grabbed the ball and raced towards Todd and Mariah, hitting Mariah on the head, calling, "You're it."

They squealed, and the game was on, each one running and bracing one arm on a tree to duck behind for protection. Mariah got Todd, who got Belle, who raced towards the shore and got Daniel, "You're it."

The five raced about being children together. Belle out of breath went back to the blanket. Daniel first grabbed up Colt and piled him on top of Belle. Then he scooped up Todd and Mariah and piled them on top of the two. He piled on all of them as they all howled with laughter together.

Colt and Mariah once again found themselves by their mother's bedside. Colt looked at Mariah, wondering if she too was seeing this. Belle slumped back against the pillow with a bright smile on her face and looked at each of her children; then she closed her eyes for the last time.

Mariah climbed into the bed next to her mother and wept on her shoulder. Colt clutched her small, fragile hand as if it was an injured bird. They wept tears of sorrow and tears of relief for the suffering Belle endured had finally come to an end. And of course, they wept for themselves.

Belle found she was no longer confined to the bed; she was walking through rugged terrain, a soldier by her side. He was in full combat gear and wearing tactical goggles that masked his face. He was strong, vigorous and alert. She wore a light summer dress, and a matching ribbon held her hair. On her feet were sandals. The sun beat down on them. He had not yet seen her.

At the moment of the blast from the Russian made 82mm mortar, Belle embraced the soldier. A barrage swept the ridge and the bodies crushed by the first blast were covered amongst the rocks and the forsaken sand. Belle surveyed the area, and went and lifted her son.

Once Todd was on his feet, he said to his mother, "Wait here a minute." And he went to look for the man who had been fifteen meters to his left. He found him, lifted him to his feet and told him, "Come on, we have a guide home." Both men made their way back to where Belle stood.

Todd wiped a smudge of dirt from his mother's face. He was no longer in uniform; now he was wearing clean trousers and a casual Hawaiian print shirt, comfortable shoes. In place of tactical goggles were Ray bans. The skyline had changed to his familiar Boston. Belle was wearing a different summer dress, clean and fresh. The smile on her face let Todd know that he had finally been taken home. He shook hands with his buddy, who began the rest of his journey home.

Colt and Mariah wept at the bedside where the used up body and mind of Belle Matherly lay.

Belle's heart was full. For thirty years, she wanted to go and find Todd. And she was finally able to make this happen. Her mother's heart could begin to heal. The question of are you hungry, are you cold that plagued her, were now forever answered.

The Carriage Driver saw them approaching. There was such a grace about the woman. She held herself up with majestic bearing. The young man walked tall and carried himself like a military man. The Carriage Driver fancied that he could always tell a military man.

Nuelle knew that she was going to be in the presence of two members of human royalty. As they reached the carriage the woman in a fresh summer dress said, "It is a beautiful night for a carriage ride, can we get a ride?"

The Carriage Driver stepped down. Nuelle swished her tail and twitched her ear. He extended his hand. First, the young man stepped on board. As Belle put her foot on the step, she let her hand open, and Todd Matherly's dog tags slipped from her hand and fell to the ground.

"Of course. We have all been waiting for you to arrive." He stepped back to his seat.

A boy of about seven walked by the carriage. He spotted the dog tags and grabbed them up and slipped the chain over his head. He proudly ran off, as a warrior, to show is friends.

In the forest, Daniel waited. Once the couple was delivered, the young Daniel that Todd remembered from childhood greeted the man his son had become when he entered the military. Belle regained her youth, her spirit, and her vibrant laugh and fulfilled her decade's goal to recover her son and bring him back to American soil.

Daniel had formed a ring of stone as their fire pit. Todd stared at their old camper, his eyes shining from so many fond memories.

His Dad popped the tab on a cold beverage and handed it to Todd. "I am ready to get some hamburgers and hot dogs going. Anyone hungry?" Daniel's eyes also were shining looking at the Belle of their youth sitting there glowing. He walked over and gave his beautiful wife a quick kiss.

Two weeks after the ceremony for Belle, Mariah's phone rang. It was Colt. "Hi, Mariah, for some reason, I have an urge to go out to the lake this weekend. We can pack up the kids and drive out there just like the old days. What do you say?"

"I say yes, I have been thinking about the lake for the past two weeks. What a great idea. I'll bring the hamburgers and hot dogs."

"I'll bring the beach ball," Colt smiled and set the phone down.

Tony, Frank, and Mike sat on the curb angry. The line drive Frank hit went straight into the tangled mess of the bougainvillea that surrounded the house at the end of the cul-de-sac. 'The Wicked House,' everyone called it. Tony thought he heard it drop into the withered ivy behind the colorful thatched thorny barrier. In the final days of summer, the last baseball they had was lost forever in a mire of neighborhood myth and legend.

The brown paint on the eaves was withered and cracked, the folding paint like eyelids, opened wide, staring out at the kids and their games. Two of the Japanese Holly along the front porch were desert dead. Field sandburs, devastating to bare feet and bike tires, spread across what was once green lawn.

The delivery van that the whole neighborhood was familiar with pulled in front of the locked gate near the far side of the property. The man climbed out, took a crate of supplies from the back of the van and carried the crate toward the gate and used a key to unlock it. He stepped inside, leaving the gate unlocked.

Mike jumped to his feet and raced toward the gate. Once inside he saw the delivery man set the crate down and knock on the front door. The door opened a sliver, and a frail hand came out holding money that the delivery man stuffed into his shirt pocket. When he turned to go, Mike ducked into the shadowy recesses of the bushes along the border of the property and waited. The delivery man walked to the gate, exited and locked the gate behind him.

The yard seemed a lot quieter with that gate locked. Tony and Frank looked at each other wondering if they would ever see their brother again. Mike, all sixty pounds of him, squatted looking around to see if anything other than the lizard near him was moving. His plan was to look for their baseball then he wondered how to get back out.

The guideposts visible from the other side of the wall were not visible from the yard. He guessed the approximate location where the line drive would have entered the deceptive thatch. Walking low to the ground, he made his way to the mess that was once ivy. He knelt down, looking and feeling around for the ball. He moved to his left and moved to the right. All the while the spindly fingers of dead ivy dragged themselves over his skinny legs extending from his summer shorts.

Some green leaves a few feet away caught his eye; the yellow flower of a dandelion was bent over. The stem was bent like an old pipe. He reached back and slapped something biting him on his leg, then crawled toward the green. That's when he saw the ball, laying there amongst the sandy colored twisted mess. He picked it up and stood up. That's when he heard the door of the house open. "Hey. You kid, what are you doing there? Come here."

Mike turned to run, but the barriers were too high, he was trapped. He looked around and tossed the ball in the direction where Frank and Tony had been sitting. The two boys heard the ball hit the asphalt and scurried towards it. Tony reached it first. He scooped it up, smiling. They turned and ran towards home, thinking Mike would follow soon.

"You deaf? It's hot out there. Come on; I just made some lemonade." The frail old woman stood there in a light dress hanging from her boney shoulders. "You're filthy, wipe your feet," she said as he reached the door. "Grab a seat over there, if you want," she pointed to an overstuffed chair with a richly patterned material depicting some far-off country lane.

Mike looked at the clean spiral rag rug in the center of the dust free floor. Behind him was a China cabinet whose dark wood glistened with fresh wax. Crystal glasses caught and bounced the setting sun rays around the room. There were oil paintings on the wall with green pastures and others with people relaxing near shorelines. The lampshades were patterned glass.

Mike squirmed in his chair. His legs itched and there was a red bug bit. He sat still when she returned from the kitchen. She carried a silver tray with a small pitcher of lemonade, two small glasses and a saucer-size plate with some cookies and placed it on a glass-covered coffee table between them.

She sat across from him, "Which one are you?"

An odd look came to his face. "Which one what?" Mike asked as she poured two drinks.

"Ah, which house do you live in?" She slowly pushed the crystal cut glass filled with lemonade towards him. "Have a cookie."

"The house on the corner just before the street that leads to the main drag. It's the green one with white trim," Mike said and took a cookie larger than his hand from the tray. Mike sat and fidgeted with the lace doily on the arm of the chair. The air in the room seemed so still. The last beams of sunlight filtered through the window, absorbing all sounds. This was not like his noisy house.

On the mantel were silver candlestick holders and a few pictures. "I think my son and your father used to play together. I thought you found your ball. Where is your ball?"

Mike took a sip of his drink. Some ran down his chin. He wiped his hand over his mouth, then thought to dry his hand on the chair then stopped. It would just have to dry sticky. "I tossed it over the bushes back to the street. My brothers know I am in here."

The fragile woman smiled at that. She knew she lived in the 'wicked house.' She lifted her glass with an unsteady hand and took a sip. "How is the cookie? I made them earlier when I saw you playing ball. I knew sooner or later one of you would be in my yard." The woman sat back in her chair. She wore a pleasant smile on her face.

Mike looked at the picture in the oval frame on the wall. The beautiful young woman in the picture had the same eyes as the woman sitting across from him and the same smile. She wore her hair in the same style. "Thank you for the lemonade and cookies," Mike said as he stood up. He wiped crumbs from his shirt and watched them silently fall to the carpet.

The lace curtains ruffled. Two beautiful angels appeared one at each side of her. One of the angels reached over and rubbed him on the head and said, "See you later Michael."

They guided the woman to the front door toward the gate. Mike followed. One Angel reached for the handle of the gate, and it opened right up. They walked through, and his little feet followed.

To Mike's surprise, a beautiful carriage was there at the curb. It was near sunset, and a dome of glowing light seemed to arch over the scene. A beautiful mare stood there in front of him, and The Carriage Driver stood there extending his hand to a woman the age of the woman in the picture with the oval frame.

Nuelle waved her tail and twitched her ear. The woman turned to Mike and said, "Thank you for seeing me home."

The chocolate, coral, amber, sky brought every photographer in Boston out. Every cell phone camera was pointed at the sky. Cats were driven off every social media in the area. It was a November dawn; the aching sky left no doubt about creation. The city bathed in a golden hue seemed lifted and many prepared for the second coming as recorded in the Nicene Creed.

Eleven year old Jamie Lee stood at the nurse's station over at Boston Children's Hospital on Longwood. Her little round hairless head was partially covered with a paisley scarf, and she imagined herself a princess wearing her pink robe. "Look. Look." She held up her iPhone with a picture of the morning sky for Nurse Adie.

"That's beautiful," she said glancing at the picture. "The sky is so beautiful this morning."

"Look close you can see the Holy Ghost," Jamie Lee offered.

Adie hoped Jamie Lee did not see the sad frown that crept across her face. She changed her face and looked up from the chart she was filling out. She leaned closer to the iPhone. "That is a wonderful picture," Adie agreed. "Can you make it over to the common room by yourself?"

"Yes," and she lowered her arm with the iPhone, took hold of the pole on the casters holding up an IV drip to her left arm plus the monitor and walked down the cool tile floors to where the other sick kids were by now. She stared at her picture wondering why Nurse Adie could not see what she saw.

Mr. Nick was the orderly in the Common Room this morning. When Jamie arrived, Jimmy was sitting reading the same book that he read yesterday. Carl was playing a game on his iPod. Dr. Steve was talking with Lou Ann's mother. Lou Ann's little smile did not match her hollow eyes.

Jamie headed for Mr. Nick, "Look at the photo I snapped from the window this morning, the Holy Ghost is there plain as day."

Mr. Nick smiled and nodded and thanked Jamie.

Jamie frowned and headed towards Jimmy. "Scoot over so I can sit to your left, it keeps this tall skateboard out of the way." He scooted; she sat down and showed him her picture.

"Do you see that?" He whispered to Jamie.

Jamie's eyes shined bright. Finally, someone else sees what I see.

"Carl, come here," Jimmy called in low tones.

Carl looked up and saw that Princess Jamie had arrived. He shut down his iPod then pushed the handle of the electric scooter and went to them. The three had formed a bond. "Good morning. No tests this morning?" he asked Jamie.

"Yes, but later after lunchtime. I can't eat until tonight. Look at this Carl," she pushed the iPhone towards him. The picture of the explosive colors of the morning sky boomed out at him.

"Email me that. I want to send it to my Mom. She always looks so down and worried every time she comes here. OK?"

Jamie took the iPhone and tapped her fingers on the screen. Carl's iPod beeped.

Carl looked and then tapped his screen. "Thank you. That cannot help but bring her a smile." Carl wondered if Jamie and Jimmy saw the Holy Ghost. He whispered to Jimmy and Jimmy nodded his head.

Mr. Nick walked over to the three, "Carl, time for us to head over to the lab." He looked at Jamie, "Can I see that picture again?"

Carl turned the scooter to go. Jimmy hopped up and gave him a hug. Then turned and helped Jamie to her feet. She bent low and wrapped her free arm around Carl's neck.

"See you later." She glanced at Jimmy. When Carl was far enough away, she said, "He is not looking too good today."

"Three Doctors were in his room late last night," Jimmy told her.

That news made Jamie queasy. Her friend Betty was taken away not long after three doctors visited her room late in the evening. She looked at her picture, and that made her feel better.

Nuelle was stationed along Longwood Street as an intoxicating blue sky pushed away the chocolate, coral, amber sky that mesmerized the morning. The earthy shades highlighted her coat. The Carriage Driver standing by Nuelle took an apple from his pocket and cut it into quarters. He fed two pieces to Nuelle and ate two. Every inch of his carriage was shiny clean, and Nuelle was groomed for a visit befitting of the King.

Carl's Mother posted the picture her son sent her to Faithbook her favorite social media. When Jamie's treatment time arrived the picture had received three thousand likes, which made Carl's Mother smile, but with tears in her eyes.

Two hours into her IV drip treatment Jamie's monitor began to beep loudly. The signal was picked up by Nurse Adie, who quickly checked Jamie's schedule and raced to the lab. The nurse in the lab was by Jamie's side; she had already called for the doctor on duty. Adie reached Jamie before the doctor. She rechecked the vital signs that the floor nurse had just checked.

Adie disconnected the IV and lifted Jamie to a gurney and clipped a pulse monitor on her finger. Jamie felt as though she had stepped into the sunshine. For the first time in forever, she was aware of that refreshing sense of the heat of the sun against her skin.

When the doctor arrived, there was no pulse. He looked into her eyes with a miniature flashlight and found no reaction in the pupils. He took a pen and wrote the time of death to conclude her chart.

Adie stared at his back as he walked away without comment. For the briefest moment, all shadows were chased from the floor that held Jamie. Carl and Jimmy noticed and held their heads down.

The Carriage Driver sat tall on his seat. Nuelle lifted her legs higher and paraded down Longwood. In the back of their carriage was Jamie. The Holy Ghost was her escort; in His wake was a stream of divine exaltation.

Looking over her shoulder He looked at the iPhone in her hand. "What's that?" He asked.

"It's my iPhone." She did not feel nervous.

"What does it do?"

"Well, you can make a phone call. You can send a text message. Depending what Apps you download you can connect to the internet, or email a picture," she told Him.

"What are those?" and His finger touched an icon. The game Bejeweled appeared. "Did I break it?"

Jamie snuggled closer. "Look, you just push here, and you can match gems or swap gems, and there is Diamond Mine or Butterflies and even Poker," she paused, "I can teach you."

He scratched His head. He reached forward touching the Carriage Driver on the shoulder. Nuelle slowed, pulled to the side and stopped.

Both the Carriage Driver and He climbed down. The two shook hands, "You are doing a fine job." He walked over and gave his rejuvenating touch to Nuelle and told her the same. He turned and said to Jamie, "I think you would make an excellent guardian angel. Do you know anyone that is in dire need of a guardian angel?" Clouds billowed and rumbled through the skies preparing for His arrival.

Her face lit the entire area. "Yes, please my Lord, my friends Carl and Jimmy."

He rubbed His chin, "Take her back."

Monday morning at 1:12 am Albert sat straight up in bed and pushed death away. He threw his feet over the side of the bed and stood. Sweat gathered on his forehead and neck. That was a week ago; he has not slept since. Albert spent his working life in a partitioned glass cubicle on a factory floor. The Plant has not heard from him since the previous Friday.

Albert had habits, many habits; he was taught to smoke early from his father. He was taught to gamble in the Marines. His family long ago left him, and now he dated a category of women that few men bothered with. He was no stranger to drinking. He was not good. He was not bad. He was not blue collar, but not quite white collar. He worked through life, and now chased by death he convulsed at his blank page. He was constrained in the squalid marshland between native intelligence and unobtainable education.

He did not go to any of his usual places; thinking that death could not find him. For the first time in his life, he entered a used bookshop. At first, he was attracted to the art books and spent many hours looking at the works of Cosimo Tura and his frescos in the Palazzo Schifanoia. He found beauty in the Allegory of April, which depicted the three graces. On the first day, the shop owner left him to browse.

The second day, Albert arrived at opening time. He ignored the art section and spent hours opening one book of poetry, reading a few words or phrases then returning it to the shelve. Once he had two volumes selected he went and sat with them in an overstuffed chair placed in the shop for that purpose.

The book shop owner observed quietly. He noted unspoken desperation that was usually seen in those entering his shop having to sell their books or the rare collection.

When Albert entered the bookshop on the third day, he was unkempt, unshaven and looked hungry. The shop owner had placed a cup and saucer on the table next to the chair alongside a copy of *Black Marigolds* by Edward Powys Mathers and a copy of poems by T.S. Eliot that included his *Four Quartets* and *The Waste Land.* Once Albert was seated, the owner filled the coffee cup, and returned to behind the counter. No words were exchanged.

At the castle which was a way station between celestial destinations the large ornate doors swung open and a man in a tuxedo strolled down the walk and looked up and down the cobblestone passageway. His worries were in regards to a guest that had been scheduled to arrive on Monday.

Albert wearing a straw fedora and a cigar stuffed in his mouth sat in the bleachers at Suffolk Downs over on McClellan Hwy. He was used to betting on the horses, but through a bookie, he never developed a taste for the beauty of the horses. His horse in the third race was in the lead rounding the last turn. He was on his feet clutching his winning tickets when dark clouds rolled quickly over the track.

Sensing his luck was about to turn he leaped two steps at a time down toward the exits. Half way down he thought of the winning tickets in his hand. He screeched to a stop next to two middle-aged women handed the closest one to him the winning tickets and kissed her on the mouth then resumed his escape. The crowd witnessing the kiss gave a hardy laugh.

When the woman recovered, she realized that she held winning tickets in her hand and smiled.

As Albert headed towards the street, he saw a black carriage with a dapper driver approaching fast. He picked up his step and ran for all he was worth toward a white carriage with a white mare waiting at a curb not too far away.

The Carriage Driver started to climb down to assist his arriving passenger. Nuelle waved her tail and twitched her ear. They both watched the man huffing and puffing his way towards them and the black carriage and black horse gaining ground.

The Carriage Driver calmly reached into his pocket and retrieved an apple. He cut it into four pieces and fed two to Nuelle and ate the other two.

The driver of the black carriage could see that it was going to be a very close race, but Albert seemed to have given himself just enough time and had enough velocity to reach Nuelle before he could get to him. Not many people cut their race that close.

The Carriage Driver started to speak and to hold out his hand to assist Albert, but then Albert without pause leaped into the carriage. The driver of the black carriage pulled up short and turned away. Behind him, the middle-aged woman and her friend were running in the direction of Albert.

"Can you get this thing going?" asked Albert looking at the two women.

The Carriage Driver seeing the final two pursuers climbed onboard and gave Nuelle her rein. "No smoking," he said, and Albert took the cigar from his lips and tossed it over. Nuelle pulled away slowly but deliberately. The two women stopped, put their hands on their knees and thought the next best thing to catch, was their breath. When that was done, they went back and cashed in his tickets.

Albert called to the driver, "Which way am I going? Are there any choices?"

"Albert, by the slimmest of margins, you have gained entry to the next level. Choices? Yes, there are choices. Many people decide to do the things they loved to do in life. From what we know about you, there might be some trouble placing you. We are going to bring you to a castle where many people are waiting." The wheels of the carriage sang their song along the cobblestone street that led towards the castle. Nuelle hearing there was no hurry took the route that went through the Commons.

The pace was slow and natural. Albert for the first time was seeing the trees and skies that were not part of his thought process when working behind the factory walls. He filled his lungs with clean air, and it was like spring nectar. He lifted his hands to his forehead and his fingers found hair. His youth was returned to him.

In the background the city receded, in the foreground, a castle warm and inviting waited. When Nuelle pulled in front, by the ornate doors, a man wearing a tuxedo walked to the side of the carriage. He glanced at the driver who was climbing down.

Once he was on the ground, he leaned over to the man you had just arrived from inside the castle and said in a low tone, "We found him at the track." Both men laughed.

Albert climbed down he shook the Carriage Driver's hand and was led inside. He was invited to dine. A woman in white brought a plate with piping hot roast beef, green peas with small white onions and garlic mashed potatoes. The music of an orchestra ensemble drifted into the room.

Albert looked around. He did not see a time clock, no presses bending metal, no florescent lights. A woman in white came over and sat across the table from him.

"You are quite different from the people who arrive. We understand that you have developed a recent interest in art. Is that true?"

Albert having just placed a shovel-sized scoop of mashed potatoes into his mouth held his hand up asking for a moment. He took a big swig from the cold beer that had been placed in front of him. "Yes."

"As it happens we have a temporary opening working on a mosaic in the great hall depicting the Final Victory. We can place you there while you determine what contribution you would be most happy making. Many of our most beautiful artisans are contributing to the project. "

Albert finished his drink and set down the icy glass. He rubbed his hands together and looked deep into the eyes of the woman in white. He said, "Let's get started."

The women in white warmed to Albert immediately. She stood, walked from the room and arranged for Nuelle to bring him the rest of the way home.

1938

Six-year-old Amy Ruth could not sleep. She lost at Jacks twice to that Becky girl down the street because she could not get past twosies. Climbing out of bed, her bare feet moved quietly along the wooden floor. She grabbed her pouch of jacks and climbed out the window.

At this hour, the streets were damp and quiet. The arch of a street lamp looked to Amy the perfect place to practice jacks. A nearby owl viewed Amy on her knees playing the game with some interest. Amy did not hear the rustling leaves or see the motion of rodents scrounging for food.

The sound of hooves and wheels clattering along the roadway were the first thing to catch her attention. Next, the smell of the smoke reached her. A breeze lifted a curtain through an open window that touched a kerosene lamp and set a house ablaze; the glow made her turn her head. Then the small screech of a rodent caught by an owl reached her. She fled to the shadows of a honeysuckle patch to hide from the night.

The clip-clop along the roadway grew closer and closer. The quiet night was shattered by screams and men rushing for water. Anyone listening carefully would have heard a murmur of prayers.

Nuelle and the Carriage Driver arrived along the lane. The Carriage Diver climbed down and held out his hand. First Amy Ruth's Mother, then Father climbed onboard. Then her uncle and two brothers and last her little sister.

The Carriage Driver walked near Nuelle's ear and whispered. He reached up and looked at a list and counted the passengers once more. Nuelle waited. When given her rein she slowly walked around the block as the Carriage Driver searched.

The men in the neighborhood were still tossing buckets of water on the relentless flames, and the mouths of women mumbled prayers wearing pain filled eyes. The passengers strained this way and that looking for Amy Ruth.

2015

Amy Ruth never really came out of the shadows of the honeysuckle bushes. Her youngest daughter, now sixty years of age herself sat on her bed reading her mother's first journal. Teardrops stained the pages.

- *1942, December Another pounding by the Sisters.*

Jewel looked at her mother lying on the bed and wondered about her life. The pages were old and rustled when turned. The first entry made with a carpenter's pencil gave the printing a heavy-handed look. *Or perhaps the look of anger,* Jewel thought. She flipped the pages.

- 1948 I *meet a man, I am pregnant. I have to tell him. What if he says no??*

Jewel closed the book, keeping her finger in between the pages. Her sister was gone now, and also one of her brothers. She wondered if she had the strength to continue reading.

- 1950 Miscarriage. *I can't breathe. I am not going to tell Bill. Oh, God.*

- 1951 *Baby brother for Kathleen. Bill has run off.*

Jewel sat the journal aside and took her Mom's hand. She tried to grasp the pain and anger that was part of her daily existence. She closed her eyes and drifted back to a time so unlike the modern day with all of its technologies. She felt her Mother was a time capsule. Her memories included running through the streets of Chicago and as a wild mare full of restless energy her only goal was outrunning her past. But the web of the streets pulled her and struggled to tame her. She picked up the journal and opened it.

- 1952 *Meet a military man. I am pregnant. The Priest tells me my thoughts are sins. He is overseas; the baby can't be his.*

Jewel tossed the journal on the nightstand. She walked out of the room so her sobs would not disturb Amy in her bed. She thought about all the journal entries that started with *Fought with* which appeared over and over. She thought about the journal entries *Miscarriage* that appeared three times and *rape, arrested*, none of which were part of the family history. Jewel thought about the entry 1964 – *I'm pregnant* (knowing that was her) and then the footnote, *five kids?* This was underlined.

- 1965 (The last entry.) *I am alone.*

Jewel's brother Clark, the one closest to her in age said he could not get away to join her. Her oldest brother William, who she barely knew, said he would drive in and could arrive possibly Monday.

Jewel thought, *I am alone.*

Back to 1938

Six-year-old Amy Ruth could not sleep. She lost at Jacks twice to that Becky girl down the street because she could not get past twosies. Climbing out of bed, her bare feet moved quietly along the wooden floor. She grabbed her pouch of jacks and went to the kitchen and climbed under the table. She saw the curtain blow inward and catch the flame. "Daddddddddddddddddddddddddd!!!!!!" she screamed, and ran to the curtains and tugged the rod to the floor.

Her father arrived and began stomping on the flames. The uncle arrived and rushed for water from the pump. Amy Ruth ran and pumped water on her burnt arm. Her mother arrived and grabbed a small braided carpet and began to pound the flames. In a few moments, the family had the fire put out as the neighbors came running in response to Amy's cry.

2015

Amy Ruth's family filled the living room and parlor. The grandchildren and great-grandchildren were there or were on their way from homes all over the country. Even many of the cousins arrived when they heard Amy was near her time. Amy's home had been filled with love and friendship, and every member of the family had benefited from her energy, wisdom, and kindness.

Jewel sat on the bed by her Mother's side. She was the youngest and as her mother aged she did not want to leave her side. When she made the call to her brothers and sisters, they all made arrangements to come and help through the final steps of her earthly journey. They wanted to be there for their mother and each other.

The Carriage Driver pulled to the curb in front of the house. So many people turned and viewed the arrival. The children went and put their hands on Nuelle. The grandchildren's eyes lit up in delight.

The Carriage Driver stepped down and extended his hand to the twenty-year-old Amy Ruth. She left the house as her family parted to make way for her. Some reached out and touched her sleeves. Her children wept seeing her young body restored.

Amy Ruth stepped into the carriage and was greeted by her mother, father, and uncle as they looked in 1938. They wanted to greet Amy and see what a tribute their little girl – the one who saved them all was getting as she departed.

"Oh, it is so good to see you all. Mom, I wished you could have met my Jewel, she reminds me so much of you. And Dad, my middle son Anthony, became a brewer following in your footsteps. I taught all of them what the two of you taught me. Be strong, fight your own battles, and be kind to those smart enough to accept your kindness."

The two woman hugged as Nuelle pulled from the curb bringing Amy Ruth home.

Audrey Lane stood and surveyed the room. The dark hardwood floors shined. The wood of her piano near the walled mirror and balance bar glowed. Her studio served as her place of work. She made her living giving piano lessons and singing lessons.

In her parlor, there was a table covered with a brocade table cloth and in the center was a polished crystal ball. On the table sat a well worn Rider Waite deck of tarot cards. On her stuffed to overflowing bookshelves were Dane Rudhayar, Aliester Crowley, H. Spencer Lewis, Ph.D., Mary Baker Eddy and of course Kierkegaard, Nietzsche, and Descartes. The Torah leaned against the Upanishads and the Rig Veda. Her heart was full.

Tonight was her woman's club. She wore only a red velvet cloak. Audrey Lane shut off the light in her studio and walked out the front door into a moonless midnight.

She drove the seven miles to the meeting place. She was very familiar with the terrain. When she first found this spot, she carried in and planted white carnations that had since grown to a rich bounty, whose fragrance filled the air about them.

Lou Ann and the six others had already arrived. Gypsy was wearing a crown gold colored cloak, not easy to obtain. Mary Jane had chosen dark blue this evening. Lou Ann wore her purple cloak; she was starting the fire in the center of their gathering. They all turned at the sound of Audrey Lane's approach, and as she stepped through the opening in the carnation plantings, she stepped out of the world of man's domain.

After their greeting, as the midnight hour began to wane, the women formed a circle around the fire. Audrey Lane removed her cloak, and the others followed. She clutched the amulet at the end of a gold chain and began their chant. The others joined in as they started to dance in a circle.

Carry me to the land beyond me; all of life cannot be in vain

Mighty spirit do ordain me; raise me up where your heart reigns

Boost my voice this moonless night; free my voice of all refrain

We will, to dance beneath your stars; with your grace, we will not abstain

The women circled the fire several times singing their chant. Then the dance ended. They retrieved their cloaks and sat by the fire catching their breaths.

Gypsy rose and retrieved the goblets and the wine. It was her turn. She handed out the glasses and poured the wine. The women talked and sipped their wine and listened to the night. The tensions of the week began to drain from them. One told of the pain she was feeling in her knee, because of a strain, and another of the strain her marriage was under.

In a bit, Audrey Lane led them in a song. Here there was no disdain. When the songs were done, they stood, and one by one gave hugs and went back to their cars. Each of the women leaving a few of their worries here in the dark with the universe and each felt less of their burdens for having participated.

Audrey Lane was the last to go. She made sure the flames were out and gathered the glasses and empty bottles and moved back towards her car. On the way home, she thought how hard it was to live a life that was not mundane and if she would have the strength to slay all the dragons that needed to be slain.

As she entered her studio she felt her first chest pain; it hit her like a runaway freight train. She lay there wondering if she would attain the next level of succession or would she have to do this all again. She looked through the door and saw a carriage pulled by a white horse with a beautiful white mane. She called through the door, "I'll be right there." But instead ran to the bath and turned on a shower that made her feel like she bathed in the rain. She pulled on some clothes, then thought it likely arcane.

The Carriage Driver stood by Nuelle he had just cut an apple into four pieces; he gave two to Nuelle and ate the other two. He was in no hurry. The Carriage Driver looked up as Audrey Lane came, as she sang across the passage between them.

As she arrived at the step of the carriage, the Carriage Driver said, "Not many arrive singing." He put out his hand and assisted Audrey Lane.

"You have to sing while the music lasts." She stepped up into the carriage. "Where do I go from here?"

"I suppose that all depends on what you believe in, doesn't it?" The Carriage Driver mused.

"Is it true that some people return as cats? Like in that movie with Jimmy Steward and that witch and warlock. You know, an animal-shaped spirit - a familiar." She waited for an answer.

"I don't know about that." He gave a quiet snort of a laugh. It had been a couple hundred years since he heard a question like that.

Nuelle was happy not many entered the carriage with thoughts of returning as an animal other than a dog.

"No really, do I have some choices?" Audrey Lane sat back against the backrest. In a moment, she was humming in contemplation.

"You do have choices. You can return again to this earthly plane. You can select to go with your peers who have gone before. Anything is within your realm. You have taught singing and piano. You have opened your studio to allow ballet dance to be taught there. You have shown great intellectual curiosity. What is your desire?"

When Audrey did not call Lou Ann to verify she got home safely, Lou Ann called her. After several attempts, she called Gypsy who lived the closest. Gypsy called for an ambulance, knowing it was no use. The deep rich color of the wood flooring seemed to fade a bit. The piano in the corner of the room did not appear to stand as straight. The reflection in the mirror seemed less bright as she was removed from her studio. Gypsy informed Lou Ann, who told the others one of their Sisters rose to the next level.

Within an hour, all seven of the women who had just sung their song to the universe gathered at Audrey Lane's studio to console each other. They held hands, then hugged and cried together.

"I can do or be anything?"Audrey Lane asked in a confiding voice.

"No one that has reached here has been denied. Not to my knowledge." The Carriage Diver told her. Nuelle waved her beautiful white tail in agreement and tossed her mane. Hearing her thoughts, Nuelle stopped beneath the glow of two gaslights.

Audrey Lane leaned forward and whispered to the Carriage Driver, even though no one was around to hear her.

An odd look came across his face, "It's never been done, but I don't see why not." He glanced at the sky waiting for thunder. But there was no thunder. He looked at Audrey's hair portraying her regal internal beast. Nuelle made a full turn in the road. Audrey Lane in her human form was no longer in the back seat.

Nuelle arrived back in front of the studio and stopped. The Carriage Driver climbed down and walked into the studio. He sat what he carried in his hand on the piano unseen by the seven women. At the doorway, he looked back into the studio. The wooden floor again had its shine. The piano stood tall, and there was warmth reflected from the mirror.

Lou Ann noticed it first. "Where did that come from?"

“It was not there a second ago,” Gypsy chimed in.

“What is it?” asked another.

Lou Ann looked carefully at the bottle. She pulled the stopper and dabbed some on her and passed it to Gypsy. Gypsy passed it on to the next until all had applied some of the liquid to their necks.

There were some words in French on the golden label. In English, it said, *Love Potion*.

The Carriage Driver stood by Nuelle. She said, "She wanted to leave all her love to her sisters here on earth."

Acknowledgement

Maria Jordan

I met Maria Jordan at Emerald Wells Café. She is funny, witty and added warmth to the atmosphere. She is a writer with a reassuring voice. Her work has been compiled into an anthology titled *The Rain and Everything,* and her children's book *Kylie's Blossoms* is a bouquet to savor. She is a natural storyteller. She shares her life experiences and the people that she has met in her nursing career with us with heartfelt charm. Throughout her stories one thing becomes clear, she loves people, all sizes, and shapes and with an abundance of compassion she assists them. She has risen above life's adversities and kept her principles intact. Her latest passion as a professor of nursing studies is flourishing.

She has offered to write an introduction to each of my self-published books. That is a sure sign of her generosity.

Acknowledgement

Genna Eastman is a professional consultant and author. She writes under the pseudonym, Genna East, for the website, Hubpages. It is a privilege to count Genna among my friends. Her writing is crafted with the utmost of care, and the subtle nature of her words draws her readers into many an enchanting journey. Her every written word seems well chosen, and when a story of hers is finished, the results are often a sculpted piece of art. She does not mind leading her readers into dark situations, but she always hands them a candle to find their way. Much of her work is available to read at no charge on Hubpages. If you are an avid reader of short stories and enjoy intricate poetry, treat yourself to a treasure chest of the written word. Be intrigued by *The Pandion Prophecy,* delighted by *Bessie*, swept away along *The Forgotten Roads of Ancient Rome*, and have your spirit lifted with *Daniel of Lucid Dreams* – a poem.

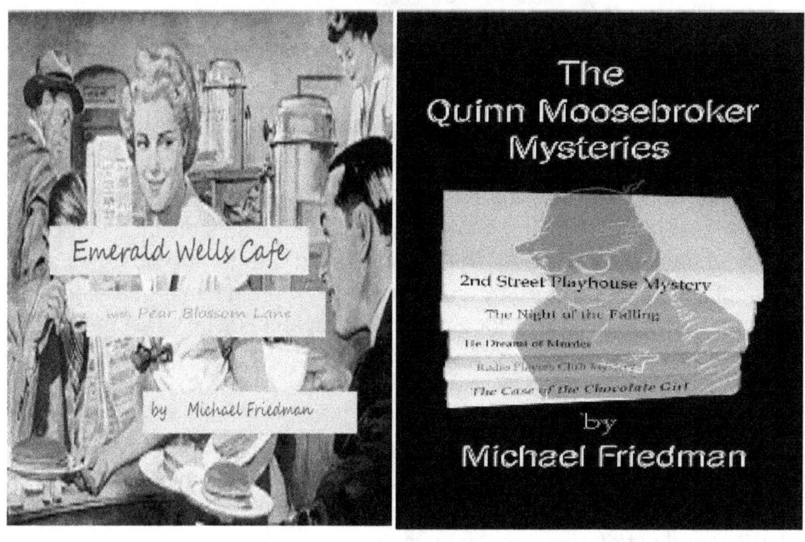

From the same author

Braids – Angel's Field

Angel is the caretaker of a way station to heaven. The guardians that prepare the girls for their final journey live in the trees of the nearby peach orchard. Everything is peaceful until a girl named Hope is found stranded at Angel's Field because her guardian has been abducted. It is up to Angel and Cyrus a woodsmen and keeper of the orchard to recover her. Joined by Carpenter from a way station for young boys called 'The Swing Zone,' the three leave their peaceful valley and set off towards the river.

Captain Castel whose daughter is very ill, is the caretaker of another way station for people going in the opposite direction across the river. Once the toll is paid, there is no return. A thief named Messr. See de Arogänt, called Seede who operates a peddler's wagon is hired by Captain Castel to bring him a guardian.

Angel, Cyrus, and Carpenter find themselves on a mission to sustain Hope.

When a rumor reaches the ears of Captain Castel that a guardian may be acquired that could save his sick daughter he sets his plan in motion. A thief named Messr. See de Arogänt, called Seede who operates a peddler's wagon is hired by Captain Castel to bring him a guardian. All appears to be going well for Seede and Captain Castel when they are found out.

A little girl is left behind in Angel's Field because her guardian has been abducted. It is up to Angel and Cyrus a woodsmen and keeper of the orchard to recover her. Joined by Carpenter from a way station for young boys called 'The Swing Zone,' the three leave their peaceful valley and set off towards the river.

Cyrus and Angel have lived a peaceful existence in their valley as caretakers of Angel's Field, a way station for young girls on their journey to heaven. Join Angel, Cyrus, and Carpenter as they make their way down the mountain and across the river in pursuit of the girl named Hope's guardian angel.

Emerald Wells Café and Pear Blossom Lane

People ask me where I am from. Since I was a Marine Corp brat, I tell them I am not from anywhere. If I could be from somewhere, it would be a place like Emerald Wells,Texas, just off the crossroads. Here you will find Earl in the kitchen of Emerald Wells Café. The owner's name is Emerald Wells, called Em by everyone in town. She does the waitressing.

Carl from Carl's Automotive stops in for breakfast every morning to say 'Hey.' He sits on the stool at the end of the counter. He likes that Em pats his shoulder the first time she passes by. He also likes to watch Gabby the owner of Let's Dress Up as she rushes across the street from her shop to the Café for her morning coffee and whatever looks good in the glass-domed dessert tray.

The Café is the center of the world for Earl, Em, Carl, Dale the Sheriff, who has known them all for their entire lives. The cast also includes the Townsends whose place is out on the highway where they tended their orchards and Tom who is retired and bought the empty gas station at the turnoff to Emerald Wells and converted it first to his abode, then The Trading Post.

The group meets monthly and shares their writing in the form of poetry readings. They call the event, Speakeasy Night. They put on their go to meeting clothes, share their poetry, eat desserts and have a good time drinking special tea out of Em's Mom's china cups.

Earl, Carl, and Jimmy served as Marines in Korea. Jimmy did not come home; Army Captain Harold Tomlin was one second late arriving in his tank to save him. Harold shows up in Emerald Wells and is so taken with Em that a courtship begins.

What genre do you ask? It's a western. It's a poetry book. It's a romance. It's a food book. It's the lost biography of the USA. In my heart, I am from Emerald Wells.

<u>The Quinn Moosebroker Mysteries</u>

Detective Quinn Moosebroker arrived in the sleepy town of Clearview Terrace, a broken man. A shootout in the line of duty killed his partner and a second bullet ended his career with the Allentown Police Department. In his forced retirement, he lives with his daughter Kate and has become a Sunday painter. His one activity is the restoration of a 1946 wood-paneled Chrysler Town and Country and an occasional trip to the local used book shop run by Blake Knightly.

Kate sets her father up on a blind date with the widow Betty Atwood to see a local play at a community theater. At the end of act one Pepper Bishop, owner of the Second Street Mystery Playhouse is murdered.

Betty Atwood starts the beginning of the best first date in history and the best thing that has happened to her in the years since her husband’s passing. The couple's casual encounter quickly develops into a partnership that unveils a pornographers scheme to sell photographs of non-consenting Clearview Terrace ladies to a big city true-detective publisher.

During Quinn and Betty’s investigation Quinn bumps heads with the local authority in the form of Detective DeLaMonte, a renegade dismissed from the New Orleans Police Department.

Eleanor Pennyworth finds Quinn Moosebroker’s name in an address book with the word ‘trusted’ written in pencil. When her partner is found dead in his Clearview Terrace home, she calls in Quinn to investigate a missing literary manuscript known as *Night of the Falling*. Quinn and Betty find themselves in a world of book people and rare book treasures.

Quinn relays a conversation about a young man's dream of murder to Betty he overheard on a quiet Saturday afternoon at the local barbershop. The story hits Betty so hard that while she tried to sleep that night she received a visitor in the form of a little boy at the foot of her bed. The haunting guest and Quinn's growing loyalty to Betty lead them to a government cover-up at a North Carolina Marine Corp Camp and to an aging Marine and his estranged wife.

On the return home, along a cold dark southern highway, Betty adjusts the Town and Country's radio and a broadcast that correctly describes the night he was shot, and his partner was killed, sends them on a detour deep into a steel town and Quinn's past. The investigation undoes Dolan Ó Braonáin a local crime boss and exposes the far-reaching tentacles of his organization.

An innocent trip to the grand opening of a Clearview Terrace thrift store and an unexpected find send this detective duo skirting along the edges of stolen Nazi loot as they do their best to find the rightful owner of a piece of art that has survived all that has come its way.

Clearview Terrace will never be the same.

I recommend

Maria Jordan's, The Rain and Everything

'The Rain and Everything' is at once a tribute, an affirmation, and a guide. The stories will reach inside you where you live. The writer's experiences are rich, and her wisdom is strong. She shares her foundation stone and the secret of her inner strength, learned at her mother's knee.

Along the way, poetry will encourage you to face life's adversities with courage. Some words trickle as soft as rain and others crackle like thunder. The style will carry you along as she relays the stories of heroes both big and small, two footed and four-footed, that she met along the way.

The wisdom of her words forms an ellipse through both the practical and the clinically mad. Her nursing career brought her face to face with the homeless and the homicidal. You will cheer her perseverance and shed tears at the injustices she encountered.

This is a volume that you will reach for often. You will ponder, and you will appreciate what is good in your world. Roll up your shirtsleeves, pour yourself a cold drink and dive in. Reading Maria Jordan is like skipping stones across a lake on a summer day. There is love and affirmation to be found between these covers.

Kimmie Thompson's, Within My Heart

This book is a collection of short stories and poems that I have written over the last few years. My heart's desire is that they will bless you, place a smile upon your face, but most of all inspire you. Some are fiction, and some are non-fiction, each carrying a special message from the depths of my heart.

Within my heart,

Lies an ocean of lost dreams,

They wait in silence.

A buried treasure,

Waiting to be discovered,

That will set my heart free.

www.ingramcontent.com/pod-product-compliance
Lightning Source LLC
LaVergne TN
LVHW010915110826
845149LV00013B/2367

* 9 7 8 0 9 8 6 0 1 1 4 5 0 *